THE
HALLOWEEN
CHILDREN

D1453029

THE HALLOWEEN CHILDREN

BRIAN JAMES FREEMAN
AND
NORMAN PRENTISS

CEMETERY DANCE PUBLICATIONS

BALTIMORE

2020

Cemetery Dance Publications
132B Industry Lane, Unit #7
Forest Hill, MD 21050
www.cemeterydance.com

First Trade Paperback Printing, 2020

ISBN: 978-1-58767-783-0

Cover Artwork and Design © 2017 by Vincent Chong
Interior Design © 2017 by Desert Isle Design, LLC

DEDICATION

We each dedicate this book to our coauthor, and to our respective spouses who put up with us while we collaborated.

We offer grateful acknowledgment to early readers Robert Brouhard and Victor Cypert; to Earthling's Paul Miller for publishing the original limited edition; to Sarah Peed, Matt Schwartz, and the entire Hydra team for giving our Halloween Children a second life as an eBook; and to Richard Chizmar for publishing this new trade paperback edition for everyone who loves print books as much as we do.

The Halloween Children
are everywhere
and they know our fears.

—written in black marker on a bench
outside the Stillbrook Apartments

Source: Digital Transcription

Names have been changed to "Interviewer" and "Victim" for the public release of this file.

Interviewer: Who are the Halloween Children?

Victim: You're missing the point.

Interviewer: Okay, if that's not the point, why did they do what they did?

Victim: You're still missing the point.

Interviewer: Was it all an elaborate hoax?

Victim: You think that's important? Then you're missing the point.

[Fifteen seconds of silence on the recording.]

Interviewer: How did you get out of there alive?

[Another silence, this time twenty seconds.]

Victim: Now we're getting somewhere, but you already know the answer to that.

Interviewer: Okay, when did you realize something wasn't right that Halloween night?

[Another silence, this time thirty seconds.]

Victim: When I discovered that so many of my neighbors were dead.

HARRIS   X

A FEW WEEKS before my entire world collapsed around me, my wife and
I rented a found-footage movie about a couple of spoiled rich kids deciding their house is haunted. They're terrified because a dish gets broken
or they hear a strange noise in their silent, spotless home.

I didn't have a lot of sympathy for them. Stuff got broken around
our place all the time, and the apartment had never exactly been quiet to
begin with.

It's called *having a family.*

I turned to Lynn at her end of the couch and I said, "If this happened
to us, how would we *know*? Seriously, how? With your Amber chatting and
singing constantly, I wouldn't be able to hear a ghost unless it screamed
right into my ear."

"You're the one talking now. Amber's asleep."

Lynn pretended annoyance that I spoke over the television, but I knew
she was miffed at the "your Amber" remark—which, let's be clear, I never
say in front of our daughter. But when my wife and I are alone, I kind of
can't resist pointing out Lynn's tendency to give Amber extra attention
and encouragement, sometimes at Mattie's expense.

Amber's the squeaky wheel.

As a for-instance: Say, after dinner, we're in the TV room and Mattie's drawing in one of his notebooks while Amber plinks away at the xylophone I could kill my brother for giving her last Christmas. She hits a ton of notes until it's like Morse code, dot-dot-dash-dot-whatever, and I swear it's like she sends her mother a coded message. *You want a cookie?* Lynn says, and Amber bright-smiles with a *Yes, please,* so you know it's just what she's been thinking, and all the while she never pauses with those sticks against the colorful metal bars, maybe practicing a sequence for her next request—you know, *Bring me a glass of milk while you're at it, okay Mom?*

And all the time Mattie's right there in the same room. "What about Mattie?" I say, and Lynn says she didn't think he wanted to be bothered while he was drawing. If he's hungry, he should speak up, she says. Then she asks him anyway, just to humor me, and Mattie looks at her like he ponders the offer, then moves his head kind of in a circle so you can't tell if he's nodding yes or no. To me, it's a sweet and sad gesture: It's like the boy thinks he doesn't *deserve* a cookie. So I'm like, "Bring him one, too. He doesn't eat it, I will."

Later, in the movie, the young wife started screaming because she heard footsteps above the bedroom ceiling.

How terrifying.

As Lynn and I watched, our new upstairs neighbor took heavy steps across the floor of his living room.

"Mr. Stompy's at it again," Lynn said. The apartment regulations said you were supposed to carpet eighty-five percent of the floors, with padding beneath, to muffle footsteps. Before I'd met the new upstairs guy in person, I thought he must weigh four hundred pounds. Actually, he was this frail little thing and I didn't know how he managed to make so much noise.

"He sounds angry," I said as he crossed the room again. My eyes tracked his movement across our ceiling. "Let's hope he doesn't start his vacuum at two a.m. again, like last week."

Next, the movie husband heard a low whisper through the baby monitor. I couldn't hear what it said because somebody used the trash chute in the hallway outside our apartment. The bag clanged against the hollow metal chute on the way down, and some glass shattered when it hit bottom.

"Some ghost has probably been trying to scare us for months now," I said. "Too bad we can't hear it."

"Shhhh," Lynn said. "Movie."

I was just joking around, of course. If my jokes had anything to do with what happened to our family that Halloween, I'm really sorry. I wish I could take it all back.

LYNN X

I HAVE NO idea how to begin this thing, this journal or whatever I'm supposed to call it.

Just having it around seems like asking for trouble.

Harris doesn't really use the computer, but what if Amber or Matt found what I'm writing for you? Their games are on here, and they're allowed to chat online with friends if we're in the room.

I thought about buying a real diary or journal, but that would be even more obvious and out of place in the apartment.

I'll probably just delete all of this anyway.

To start, you said I should write a little bit about myself, as if you and I hadn't already had a couple of sessions.

So here goes nothing:

My husband, Harris, is the handyman for the apartment complex we live in, although sometimes I think he isn't very handy at all.

My daughter, Amber, is exceptionally talented at everything she tries.

My son, Matt, is a lot like his father.

I work as a computer tech support operator for ComQues, a job that I can do remotely from home with a VoIP phone program the company provided me and remote-access software that allows me to view the customer's computer.

My job is simple, but I'm also very good at what I do.

Most computer stuff can be fixed in one of four ways, and most people are so grateful when you solve their problem.

Once in a while you get some grumpy Gus, but I know how to handle them. If you talk nice to them, they eventually calm down.

Honestly, they're just frustrated because their machine doesn't do what they expect it to.

Almost as bad as people sometimes—ha!

But none of this really explains why I'm seeing you, does it?

You also asked me to write down my thoughts and feelings between our sessions so we could better discuss them, right?

Well, right now I'm thinking maybe a woman in a strong marriage shouldn't be seeing a marriage counselor alone, in secret, without her husband knowing.

I've been thinking about that a lot since our first session.

But what you *really* want me to do is answer the question you asked me at the end of our last session, right? The one I didn't want to answer?

You asked what about Harris annoys me the most.

The reason I didn't want to answer is simple: Just like how someone in a good, stable, happy marriage shouldn't be visiting a marriage counselor on her own, she also shouldn't have to prioritize as many answers to that question as I had running through my head.

Then again, you already knew that, didn't you?

Hence this diary. Or journal. Or whatever.

I guess I'm really doing this, and I guess it's okay to type this since I'll probably just delete it.

Here's the answer to your question:

One of the biggest annoyances is how much Harris shelters Matt.

How exactly will Matt grow up to be a real man if his father is always holding his hand and serving the world to him on a silver platter?

In fact, Harris does the exact opposite with Amber. It's almost like he doesn't even know our daughter exists some days. It's Matt *this* and Matt *that*.

But you know what's really bugging me right now?

It's actually nothing to do with Harris. Not exactly. It's what his son is up to when I'm not looking.

You see, I think Matt is sneaking around this apartment and moving things, just a little bit, for reasons I can't quite figure out.

For example, I like to read in bed to help me wind down after a long day, and right now I'm reading *Rebecca* by Daphne du Maurier for about the hundredth time.

But last night, when I went to bed, the bookmark was in the wrong chapter.

I asked Harris about it and he insisted he had no idea.

He's never lied to me, at least not that I know of, so that makes me think of Matt.

Why's my son sneaking into our bedroom?

It's like he's testing me to see if I notice.

I don't like that. Not one little bit.

Another example of Matt being up to no good:

Every evening we have what we call "family time" in the living room.

I might be surfing the news on my phone.

Harris is probably playing Candy Crush or some other time killer of a game on his.

Amber is either chatting with her friends on the computer or playing her xylophone.

Matt is always drawing in his notebooks.

Always.

But the thing is, sometimes I feel like maybe he's not really drawing at all.

I think he's watching me out of the corner of his eye, just to see what I'm doing.

I don't know why he would be spying on me, and I never actually catch him in the act, but why else would I feel like he's watching me if he wasn't actually doing it, you know?

I also don't like *that* one little bit.

HARRIS X

"**M**Y SIDE," Mattie whispered to me one day. His mom and Amber were in the community lounge fixing up a craft project for fifth-grade history—a shoe box, construction paper, Popsicle sticks, and a toilet-paper tube with eyes drawn on it, and *voilà*, you've got a scene from *The Call of the Wild* or something. The girls were busy, in that conspiratorial way they have, and my big-dad fingers were apparently too clumsy to be trusted with rounded scissors or delicate wisps of cotton pulled into clouds, so I was banished to the TV room. Mattie caught me during one of the commercial breaks.

(And do I need to point out how courteous that is? Even if the show isn't any good—a *Star Trek* spin-off with the wrong cast, or those stupid contestant interviews on *Jeopardy!*—Mattie will always wait for the commercial instead of interrupting. If we're watching a DVD, he's patient until I push the pause button. I'd like to say I taught him to do that, but he figured it out on his own. Amber's still learning, I guess. Lynn, too, for that matter.)

Anyway, I followed him to the bedroom he shared with Amber.

When Mattie said "My side," since we were alone, I was tempted to respond: "Of *course* I'm on your side, Buddy, you know that. No matter what." There's nothing wrong with a parent saying that. It's being supportive. To be careful, I could have added, "I'm on your side, and I'm on Amber's, too"—even though Mattie tended to be the more reasonable, nine times out of ten. Ten out of ten.

Then I realized he wasn't asking me. He was telling.

His side.

It would take only one picture of the kids' bedroom to explain. Mattie's bed was made. His books were arranged on each shelf, the Harry Potter and other series books together in order, paperbacks aligned neatly according to size, and a small section on the top right for schoolbooks and his dictionary. A gooseneck lamp sat on his wooden desk, with one sharpened pencil in the groove along the desk's back edge—more pencils and supplies were stored in the drawer, to be brought out only when needed. The same was true of his toys, closed in the bottom dresser drawer, awaiting rare occasions when Mattie chose to play rather than read or draw.

Amber's side, well…we wouldn't want to stifle her creativity by insisting on order, would we? The covers were kicked aside, with last night's clothes in a heap on the bedside floor. Two of her four dresser drawers were perpetually open, and a clump of cotton swelled over the sock drawer, looking like it had been slammed to catch someone's toes. Amber's schoolbooks were along the windowsill, on or under the bed, or buried beneath stuffed animals or other toys that populated her side of the room.

Her side. On TV comedies, fighting siblings sometimes chalked a dividing line down the middle of their carpet, or hung a string across the bedroom, clothes draped over it to create an improvised curtain. *I'm mad at you. Keep your stuff on your side of the room, Cindy Brady or Todd Huxtable or whoever.* Mattie and Amber never needed to draw the line. Her stuff overflowed and created its boundary—mess as a territorial marking. Mattie's neatness was the border guard. Nothing crossed over.

Except something did. That's what Mattie wanted to show me.

He didn't need to point it out. One of Amber's dollhouse figures had clearly intruded onto Mattie's side of the room and lay facedown on the carpet. The dollhouse was an extravagant gift from Grandfather

Chitwood, on Lynn's side. It opened up like a suitcase to offer cutaway views of a single-family home with four bedrooms, two baths, a fully stocked kitchen, a dining room, and an entertainment center. An attic playroom and a full basement. The dollhouse was too heavy for Amber or even Lynn to carry; whenever Amber wanted to play with it outside or in the community lounge of our apartment complex, we had to stuff all the little people inside, along with all the removable furniture and the two cars for the garage, and I'd lug it around for her. If our family could afford to take vacations to Europe or on cruise ships, I guess that's how heavy our suitcase would be.

I'd drag it around wherever she wanted me to. Sometimes, after all my effort, she'd hardly play with the dollhouse.

It ended up back in the kids' room, as usual, hinged open with the whole mini-household suffering from the aftereffects of an earthquake. Hurricane Amber, to be more accurate. Plastic chairs and lamps now lay on their sides in the cutaway rooms, and a sofa and dining room table had spilled onto the carpet. From an upstairs bedroom, the bed had shifted from the back wall and hung precariously over the open edge, perhaps ready to bedknob-and-broomstick into space like in that Angela Lansbury movie. The residents themselves occupied separate rooms of their spacious and disorderly home, stiff-postured in some strange tableau or other. My favorite was one of the plastic teenagers, which Amber had kneeled next to an upstairs toilet as if it heaved up penance after a night of binge drinking. Meanwhile, a diapered infant the size of my thumb lay unattended in the garage, its head near the back wheel of the family SUV.

Amber might have intended some story line to her placements, or she might have arranged the figures absentmindedly. Who could say? At least all the family members stayed on their own property—even the pets, with an unleashed poodle in the attic and the cat figurine curled snug atop an overturned refrigerator.

Except for the head of household. That's what Mattie had called me up here to see. The father figurine—the one Amber called Mr. Man— was bent into a crawling position. Perhaps the hurricane had blown him out the top-floor bedroom, but he didn't seem in any hurry to return to his family. He was aimed away from the dollhouse and had crawled into Mattie's side of the room.

To reinforce his point, Mattie traced the room's unspoken border with the toe of his shoe. "Her guy shouldn't be on my side."

"I know, son. Question is, what are you gonna do about it?"

That surprised him, I could tell. I guess he expected me to take action: call his sister up here and yell at her, maybe bring his mom into it, too. Instead, I decided to give Mattie a few things to think about. Maybe help teach him to stand up for himself now and then.

"You could just put it back," I told him. "That'd be the easiest solution. No need to make a fuss. You wouldn't even have to bend down to pick it up. Simply nudge Mr. Man with your foot until he's back on Amber's side of the room."

Mattie nodded—that kind of circle nod he did, where it wasn't clear if he meant yes or no.

"Easy in the short term," I said. "But Amber probably wouldn't even notice. Your mom cleans up after your sister all the time, and now you'd be doing the same thing. Is that what you want?"

"She'll just do it again," Mattie said.

"There you go."

Mattie scrunched up his face. I could tell he was thinking hard, but he didn't say anything. I waited awhile before I decided to help him a bit.

"You know, some countries have this official border crossing." The metaphor had been in my mind for some reason, so I decided to go with it. "You need to get permission to cross into the country, with official documents. At the gate there's maybe bloodhounds and armed guards and such. If you do things according to the rules, there usually isn't a problem. You understand?"

He waited for me to continue.

"But sometimes people don't follow the rules. They don't have permission, so they sneak across at night, when the gate is closed. Or, they find a different place to cross where the guards can't see them. Sometimes, though…sometimes these people get caught. What do you think happens to them? Do you think they're just sent home with a pat on the back?"

"I don't know," Mattie said.

"Look at it this way: If you're *nice* to Mr. Man after he broke the rules, then isn't that the same as telling him the rules don't matter? And not just him, since the rest of Mr. Man's family is watching. If he gets away with it, they know they can get away with it, too."

Mattie looked at Mr. Man. He considered the dividing line across the bedroom and the stray multitude of toys and clothes on Amber's side.

"Your choice," I told him.

As I left the room, I heard a grunt and the snap of plastic as Mattie's shoe stomped into the carpet.

EMAIL FROM
JESSICA SHEPARD

From: Jessica Shepard
To: Jacob Grant

WELL, YOU wanted me to tell you all about my "new life" here in Maryland, and since you're never on Facebook anymore and you still won't replace your broken phone on "principle" because you blame the bus driver for it being broken, I figured an email would have to do the trick.

I'm living in this place called Stillbrook Apartments. It's only a few blocks from campus, which is great. This complex isn't as pretty as it looked in the photos on their website, but I guess that's to be expected.

There are a dozen brick buildings surrounded by a green lawn and tall trees that have probably been here since before the apartments. In fact, it kind of looks like an extension of the college campus if you didn't know better.

There are six apartments in each building, two on each floor. My apartment isn't as nice as the one on the website (again) or even the model apartment in the leasing office. We have a laundry room in our building, though, and a big lounge area in the basement. Not all the buildings have that, so it almost makes up for the small apartment. Almost.

I actually went back to the leasing office to make sure they hadn't given me the wrong keys when I opened the door to my apartment and saw how small it was, but the lady who works there was already out to lunch and I never saw her come back that day. Her name is Shawna and she seems to take a lot of long lunches. I'm not exactly sure what she does here, so I'm thinking she might be related to the owners or something.

I've already met the handyman twice. He's this middle-aged dude named Harris, and he lives one building over with his wife and kids. Really nice, but I don't think he's an actual handyman by trade, because he still hasn't fixed the noise I keep hearing in the walls at night. It's like there's something whining in there, but the more I think about it, the more I think the sound is coming from the apartment upstairs, which is kind of weird because it's vacant right now. Or supposed to be. (Cue scary music!)

In all seriousness, I kind of feel like there's a lot of odd things around here that I wasn't expecting.

Like there's this woman who might be faking a disability to rip off her old employer or maybe an insurance company. At least that's what everyone says. She lives on the floor above me, and the one time I bumped into her in the hallway she was moving like she was in slow motion, but she looks pretty young to be having any kind of mobility problems.

So, yeah, there are definitely some "features" the fine folks who own Stillbrook Apartments didn't mention on the website, which makes me wonder what else might be happening around here!

Gotta go, late for class. Will email soon. Or you could, you know, join Facebook like everyone else. I'm posting tons of pics. Love you!

—Jess

HARRIS   X

THE FOLLOWING morning, I stopped in the leasing office for my daily printout of tasks. Sometimes there's nothing, sometimes there's two pages (especially after the weekend), but mostly it's a small Excel list, with building and apartment numbers in the first thin columns, then the resident's complaint or problem in the wider blocks. Shawna will type her own comments on occasion—what she told the tenant or what solution she thinks I should try—but that's mainly so she feels like she's a boss. I always know what to do.

It's worth clarifying that I wasn't a janitor. I didn't do the lawn service, either, or anything with plumbing or internal wiring. Stillbrook Apartments hired contractors for those kinds of jobs: Standard practice was to call whoever's cheapest and hope they'd be quick about it. I basically ended up with the smaller tasks—stuff that supposedly didn't need "expert" attention. I'd fix a fallen shelf here and there, oil a door, change a fuse or hallway lightbulb; lay down mousetraps or set off a roach bomb; easy cover-ups with paint, window caulk, or tub sealant. I might turn off the water on an overflowing toilet or put a bucket beneath a roof leak until the professionals bothered to show up.

Basically, I was the on-site guy for the eight apartment buildings in our complex.

It gives you an idea what kind of place I'm talking about when I mention my job was part-time, with no benefits. With nearly a hundred apartments, each one bringing in a thousand-plus dollars each month, you'd think they could have hired a full-time handyman.

Sure, there wasn't *always* a lot for me to do—sometimes it was nothing—but after a holiday weekend or some random alignment in the stars, this place would go crazy with complaints. To make up for the slow days, I told Shawna I'd do the grass cutting, some of the minor electrical and plumbing repairs. Then they could take me on full-time. I'd get health insurance and paid vacation, and with my extra pay Lynn could cut back her tech-support hotline hours.

Shawna's answer was always the same: "It's not in the budget."

And yet *her* job was full-time, and I guarantee Shawna wasn't busy all day. Everybody's rent money funded her time with online crossword puzzles and Bejeweled on Facebook, plus lengthy personal phone calls. Oh, and these management conferences she attended twice a year. She'd come back with a suntan and new ideas: a resident satisfaction survey, an ice-cream social for the younger tenants, a monthly newsletter she wrote for three months, then abandoned. These conferences were also her source of authority for impromptu policy decisions: "I've spoken with managers in other communities, and they're all adding the same processing fee" or "I attended a workshop on this issue, and for legal reasons we can no longer accept package deliveries in the leasing office."

When I stopped in that October morning, Shawna quickly minimized something on her computer screen. Too late, since I'd already heard the click of a five-jewel match when I pushed open the front door.

Like with most small apartment communities, our leasing office was simply a ground-floor unrented apartment with an office desk in the front room and the remaining space decorated as a model unit. High-wattage bulbs ensured all the rooms were bright and welcoming, and some consultant helped pick soothing colors for curtains and bedspreads, with accent pillows for the living room sofa and chairs. Because the furniture was mostly unused, it stayed clean, and the flowers were plastic, so they always looked fresh. The television and stereo equipment were those cardboard stand-ups you sometimes find in furniture stores: "Yeah, we don't sell TVs, but here's what one would sorta look like on this entertainment stand."

Shawna smiled as I entered—the same smile she gave potential renters, and equally sincere, I'm sure. As always, she was well put together, like the display rooms: professional, solid blue dress, with a gold spiral brooch for accent; hair pulled back from her face and a modest coating of blush and lipstick. She had my work list already printed out and at the top of her IN tray, and without rising from her chair she handed it to me across the desk.

Only a handful of tasks appeared on the page, but she called my attention to the first item. "All" was listed in the building and unit columns, with "Distribution of flyers" in the explanation box. Shawna then handed me a filled manila envelope with a single orange sheet taped on the outside to identify the contents. "Hand-deliver one of these to every door," she said. "And pin one to each of the building's announcement boards."

Hand-delivery, meaning *my* delivery, was Shawna's favored means of "official" communication. It saved the cost of a stamp, but, more important, it saved her from actual contact with residents. No immediate follow-up questions, as she'd get on the phone. And with email, you could never be sure the message didn't fall into someone's spam filter. Legally, as she supposedly learned in one of her seminars, a hand-delivered note was nearly as good as a certified letter.

I examined the outside of the envelope, reading the first few lines of the flyer. "Oh, my kids aren't gonna like this."

"Can't be helped."

"There's still two weeks. The families could take up a collection."

Shawna shook her head back and forth. "It's not just money. See, if we have a party in the public area, it means Stillbrook has sanctioned it. We could be held responsible if anything went wrong. *Legally* responsible."

Hard to miss that emphasis on her favorite word. "That's ridiculous. There'd never be parties if that's the case. The kids love the Halloween party. We can decorate the lounge ourselves, and the food can be potluck..."

"All part of the problem, I'm afraid. At Terrace Green in Jersey City two years back, a resident fell off a ladder while hanging a black crepe streamer. She sued the management company and won—with the settlement costs eventually passed along to other residents in the form of rent increases. Would you want that?" Shawna didn't wait for my answer. "At one high-rise community in Tampa, people got E. coli poisoning from a spoiled-meat appetizer provided by one of the tenants—guess you would call it a potluck surprise—and the reputation of the building suffered as a result."

I barely listened to her when she got like this. I knew she was practicing on me, so the excuses would sound even better when she repeated them. As she listed a few more party-going disasters, I stood there and read the memo in full.

NOTICE: Due to limited funds, unfortunately there will be no community Halloween party this year.

As a safe alternative, we will allow trick-or-treating within our neighborhood, on a limited basis.

Rules for the evening of October 31 are as follows:

• No distribution of unwrapped candy.

• No fruit or homemade baked goods.

• Respect your fellow tenants: Children may knock on doors between the hours of 7:00 p.m. and 8:30 p.m. ONLY.

• No paper decorations on doors, as these can be a fire hazard.

• Only plastic pumpkins are permitted. In previous years, fresh pumpkins have been smashed in the street or parking lot, causing cleanup problems.

• Do not hang decorations from the courtyard trees.

• No in-ground decorations, as these create a hazard for our lawn crew.

• "Think before you Trick": No vandalism of any kind will be permitted.

Finally, adult guardians **must accompany and supervise their underage children** during all trick-or-treat visits. To participate in this holiday event, the adult guardians must sign and return this form to the leasing office, waiving Stillbrook Apartments of any legal responsibility pursuant to damages or injuries that may result from the evening's festivities.

Print Name   Signature   Date

Print Name   Signature   Date

The more I read the memorandum, the angrier I got. I pictured Shawna taking notes at one of her stupid legal workshops. Afterward, scouring the Web for further anecdotal evidence to support her arguments. Cutting-and-pasting rules and legal language she could apply to the Halloween situation, supplemented with her own small-minded ideas.

This should be a holiday for the kids to enjoy. It wasn't fair to take it away from them, especially while pretending you were doing it for their own good.

Besides, the idea of restrictions never quite appealed to me. It's like putting a loose cap on a liter of soda pop, then daring people to shake the bottle.

Things are bound to explode.

I GUESS you're wondering what all of this has to do with what happened. *Get to the point, Harris.* Right?

Let me take a stab at answering.

I'm no expert, but I think the environment in our apartment complex had *everything* to do with what happened.

Not just our management policies and our neighbors, but maybe even the issues that had been simmering within my own family.

You go through life thinking you're essentially invincible, the star of your own personal little movie, and then from out of nowhere you're tossed into chaos that you can't predict or control.

When this sort of thing happens, you have to make perfect decisions from imperfect information or you might just end up in a padded cell, talking to a headshrinker who thinks you can tell him where the bodies are hidden.

I don't know.

At least, I don't think I do.

There's a lot I remember about that Halloween, but the last hour, the minutes leading up to midnight when the fire department was kicking down doors and everyone was screaming—so loud, all of those horrendous cries—and the police were shouting...

Well, there's not a lot I remember about *that*.

I might have done any of the things they say I did.

Or none of them.

But that's why I'm making these recordings, isn't it?

Let's find out.

LYNN   X

TO BE safe, I'm going to call you Mr. Therapist in this file. I hope you don't mind.

Or should I call you Doctor?

Either way, I don't want to use your real name, since I can't be certain someone else won't find this little homework assignment.

You want to know about the problems I see in the marriage?

A major one is that Harris doesn't even realize how destructive his son can be.

I know for a fact that Matt has broken Amber's toys on purpose.

You wouldn't think the boy had it in him, not that scrawny little kid, but Matt has a temper.

I haven't exactly seen it, but I've found the destruction left in his wake.

I also think Matt tries to sabotage things around the house, like the time someone loosened the hot water connection under the kitchen sink, which would have been a huge mess if I hadn't been there when it disconnected.

When I've pointed these incidents out to Harris, he denies the mere possibility of Matt causing trouble.

He says it's just as likely that the neighbor upstairs did something to Amber's toys, maybe more likely.

What a load of crap.

Have I told you about the neighbor upstairs?

Harris has all of us calling him Mr. Stompy, but I think Amber originally came up with the nickname. Isn't that cute?

His real name is Mr. Johansson, and I've only met him once, but I'll never forget that meeting because it was such a bizarre afternoon.

The kids were at school and Harris was at work, and I thought I'd surprise everyone with a cake.

A real Coconut Pound Cake, made from scratch, like my mother made when I was a kid growing up on the farm.

This wasn't something I'd normally do, but, to be honest, that morning Harris had made a joke about me being addicted to my "As Seen on TV" kitchen contraptions, so I wanted to remind him that I could really cook if I wanted.

I walked to the corner store to get my ingredients, including real cake flour like mom would have used, not all-purpose flour.

I borrowed a stand mixer from Mrs. Tammisimo, one of the other mothers in this complex, who chewed my ear off for a good half-hour about all of her favorite cakes before I could delicately excuse myself and get to work.

I followed the recipe my mother had jotted down in the back of the only cookbook I own, *The Joy of Cooking*, which had been her wedding gift to us.

After mixing everything together, I poured the well-creamed mix of eggs, sugar, flour, shortening, vanilla extract, and coconut into our only cake pan, popped it into the preheated oven, and then went to pour myself a glass of wine and sit on the couch to celebrate my achievement.

I should have looked in the oven more closely.

Five minutes later, smoke was pouring out of the kitchen and the smoke detector was blaring like a stuck pig.

I spilled my wine in my hurry, jumping off the couch, and I threw open the oven door and quickly found the source of the smoke: not my cake, but the dozen green army men *someone* had hidden on the back of the bottom rack.

Now, who could that have been, right?

I didn't even know Matt owned army men, but Amber certainly didn't and even if she did, she wouldn't have done something as stupid as putting plastic toys in the oven.

By the time I extinguished the small fire and opened all of the windows, the smoke detector was silent again, but the shuffling feet upstairs certainly were not.

These were heavy, angry steps.

Then came the pounding from above: *thump, thump, thump.*

As if upstairs guy had a cane and was using it to make a point.

Thump, thump, thump.

I have to admit, this pissed me off.

Not only was the cake ruined, and not only had my son pulled another one of his stupid pranks on me, but now the jerk upstairs was making a ruckus to prove some stupid point about the noise, which was ironic because *he* was the noisy upstairs guy.

Thump, thump, thump.

My patience was already at my limit, and I realized that if he did it one more time, I was probably going to go up there and give him a piece of my mind.

But then I heard something else, something that kind of freaked me out.

It almost sounded like a voice whispering: *Help me.*

I looked around the apartment, thinking maybe I was hearing a neighbor's television or radio.

Help me.

And then:

Thump, thump, thump.

Finally, I understood: Something was wrong with upstairs guy and he was trying to get my attention!

I ran out the front door of my apartment, down the hallway, and up the stairs two at a time, feeling like a horse's ass for my overly critical thoughts that had been pointed in my neighbor's direction just seconds earlier.

What if he was dying? What a great neighbor I was, right?

I pounded on the door and yelled, "Are you okay? I'm here to help!"

A long time passed, and I stood there thinking about all of the various bad things that could have happened to our Mr. Stompy—heart attack, stroke, intruder—until finally I heard the lock being turned and the door swung open.

A small, bookish man stood there, his eyes enlarged by Coke-bottle eyeglasses the likes of which I thought vanished in the 1960s.

"Are you okay?" I asked, out of breath.

"Of course I am, Mrs. Naylor. Are you?"

"How do you know my name?"

"It's on your mail, which the cursed mailman often puts in my box by mistake, of course. You and your family are the tenants of the apartment directly below my humble home. My name is Mr. Johansson."

I laughed, realizing that I had again instantly thought the worst thing possible about upstairs guy.

Of course he knew our names from the frequent mail mix-ups.

If you came in the front door and found your misdirected mail sitting on the table in the lobby, that was due to the kindness of a neighbor who didn't drop it in the trash can, which was closer.

"Mr. Johansson, this will probably sound silly, but were you just whispering 'Help me' through the floor?"

"My dear," he said with a giggle, "I try not to ever whisper anything to the floor. You never know who might be listening in an old building like this. Would you like to come in for a spot of tea?"

I considered his offer and then politely declined, deciding we had probably gotten to know each other well enough for one day.

But later, when I was lying awake that night, unable to sleep thanks to Harris's snoring, I thought about the voice I thought I had heard.

Where could it have come from?

HARRIS   X

A S I was taking around those Halloween notices, I mentally rearranged
the other tasks so I could complete them along the way. If I planned
ahead like this, it kept me from having to double back.

Besides, posting the notices was always more of a nuisance than you
might think. In addition to taping one to each door, I was supposed to
pin one to the announcement board in every building. These boards hung
next to the mailboxes in each entryway, and they were covered with a
locked panel of sliding Plexiglas. God forbid that anybody could easily
post a "Babysitter Available" flyer or "Computer Desk for Sale" page with
tear-off phone number tabs. No such luck. Shawna didn't want that kind
of foolishness to get confused with her official proclamations.

Except it didn't take a brain surgeon to circumvent her security
measures. People would tape their own messages on the outside of the
glass—frequently covering up Shawna's notices beneath. Or they would
slide a homemade flyer behind the glass panel, hoping it would land faceup on the locked side.

And guess who was supposed to clear away these unauthorized post-
ings? Well, I'd do it in a halfhearted way, at least to make sure the latest
Stillbrook memo got clear viewing for a day or so. An hour or so.

In building four, I pulled one of the flyers from Shawna's envelope. As usual, the stupid little key-and-ratchet lock didn't work so well, so I had to stand there and jiggle and rattle the thing until it unlatched, then scrape the Plexiglas aside to get to the corkboard. I crumpled away some index cards advertising a local cleaning service, thumb-tacked the Halloween notice, then closed and relocked the plastic covering. The front Plexiglas was speckled with torn corners of paper beneath bits of tape residue, but the trick-or-treat memo was mostly legible through the clear plastic—including the consent lines at the bottom, which struck me as funny, since nobody'd be able to get past Fort Knox to sign this particular copy.

I was heading to the top floor for Joanne Huff's latest repair issue when a loud screech nearly made me drop my toolkit. It was a horrible noise like grating metal and a terrified child shrieking beyond language, as if a kid's hair got caught in the gears of some bladed farm implement and he was being pulled into its grinding teeth.

I'd heard the sound before, of course, but it always startled me whenever I was this close. I don't know how the other residents could stand it.

Marie and Todd Durkins on the ground floor owned this ugly, exotic bird. Some variation of macaw or parrot or cockatoo, but according to Shawna this one supposedly cost them a thousand dollars. They really overpaid, though, since it was supposed to learn and repeat clever little phrases, but all it did was squawk like it was being tortured. The identical awful noise, every time, but you could *never* grow used to it. The sound occurred randomly, and just when you'd forgotten about it—settled into some elusive calm after dinner, or drifted toward a satisfying sleep—well, *that's* when another half-human screech intruded and startled you into a brief panic. It must have been some kind of primal reaction, because I swear just about every time I'd think, *It's a child. Oh, God, some poor child's been hurt...*And then a split second later I would catch myself and remember, *Shit, it's just that damn bird again.*

Right there, right outside the Durkinses' door? Scared me, yeah, and it was also like somebody had jammed knitting needles into my eardrums.

Thing is, we're not allowed to have pets at Stillbrook. The Durkinses got away with it, though, since for some reason Shawna defined pets as cats or dogs, period. Maybe bigger things, too, like horses or Galapagos tortoises or something. Unit A in building seven has a rabbit that's allowed—I had no problem with that decision, since I'd never seen or heard the twitchy-nosed critter—but this squawking terror was another matter. If the Durkinses can have that bird, why couldn't Amber and Mattie get a cat, or a small dog, as long as it's not too yappy? Well, when I asked, I got some anecdote about how "in River View, one of those innocent puppies destroyed the carpets and the kitchen cabinets, and even a monthly pet fee wasn't enough to cover the damage when the tenants moved out, blah, blah, blah."

This is a little embarrassing to admit, but here goes. We were kinda helpless with the rules and things, considering how inflexible Shawna was, and sometimes it brought out a little mischief in me. Stillbrook was a small enough development, which meant I pretty much knew people's schedules and what their cars looked like in the main lot—so I could always gather who was home during the day and who wasn't. If I knew the Durkinses were out, and the floor above was clear as well, I'd attempt a little vocal training on that bird.

I've always loved those jokes about a parrot cursing during a fancy dinner party or when the preacher or Queen of England visits. It's pretty funny imagining a snooty old royal or some sanctimonious blowhard's shocked reaction after getting cussed out by an ill-trained pet. The humiliated owners trying to apologize, too, saying Birdie's *never* said such things before...and all the while the parrot keeps repeating *Suck my this* and *Stick it up your that.*

The Durkinses' bird never learned a word from its owners, but who's to say it might not respond to another voice? So I'd maybe speak into their keyhole or cup my hands against their door and whisper into the wood. A few playground-style words, real immature-like. An f-bomb once or twice was probably the worst I ever did. And a few phrases I'd imagine the bird speaking aloud. "Polly's a twat." That kind of thing.

Probably more for my own amusement than anything else. I didn't expect I was ever loud enough for the bird to hear.

But this time, that Halloween flyer had me thinking in terms of trick-or-treat. If someone's not home, you're supposed to get revenge on them—and God knows the Durkinses and their damn bird needed some comeuppance for that awful nails-down-the-blackboard screech you could hear throughout the neighborhood. My righteous indignation made me a little bolder.

I'd never crossed this line before, but I carried a master key as part of my maintenance job. I could get into anybody's home when they weren't there.

I looked at the deadbolt. Lifted my key ring.

Not really a risk, as long as I did something subtle. The Durkinses would never trace it back to me. Might not even discover it right away. At least, not until the preacher visited.

Even if I was caught in the act, I could hold up my task list and say I got the apartment numbers confused. *Whoops. No wonder the kitchen bulb was fine—I thought I was in building seven...*

I slid the master key in place, turned it to the left.

Click.

The same key worked in the door handle. I turned it, heard the latch pop on the inside knob.

A wave of anxiety swept over me. The bird's piercing squawks were rarely isolated. There'd likely be a few more to follow, perhaps even a machine-gun burst of high, shrill cries. If that awful klaxon blasted while I was inside the Durkinses' apartment—louder because I was closer, because I'd stepped into a place where I didn't belong—I think I might have had a heart attack. It would be like walking toward a ticking bomb, unaware when it might decide to explode. I'd cross the living room toward the wire-domed cage, covered with a black cloth to trick the bird into thinking it's nighttime—as if that would stop the random cries, as if anything could stop those cries. Forget the cloth, then, let's say the cage was uncovered, beady bird eyes following my movements, a feathered head tilting to the side to watch me through the bars, dirty wings twitching and the body swaying on its perch as the animal takes in a deep breath, prepared to...

"*Harris!*"

Sweet Christ, the damn thing knew my name. It shouted—

"*Harris! Is that you?*"

Not as loud as the bird, but nearly as shrill. Coming from the third floor. Mrs. Huff.

My hand was still on the knob. I hadn't turned it.

Joanne Huff. On my task printout, her entry read as unit F, building six. Complaint: rattle in bathroom heating duct.

"Be right there." I locked the Durkinses' apartment, then made my way up the stairs.

"I thought I heard you. Called the office yesterday afternoon, so I knew you'd be here." Joanne adjusted her speech as I got closer, as if she could intuit my exact position on the staircase, then push just enough into her voice to reach me. Her whole philosophy of life was like that, really: locating the point of minimal effort. "I can't come to the door, so let yourself in. Use your keys."

Why couldn't Joanne open her own damn door? Maybe she was still getting dressed, wet from the bath or shrugging into a nightgown. Maybe she was on the toilet and I'd hear a muffled flush as I unlocked her front door. Of course, she wanted everyone to believe she was an invalid, but her neighbors all knew better. It was rare to spot her outside the apartment, but on those occasions she always looked healthy enough, if a bit slow-moving. Joanne was in her mid-thirties, tall and a little clumsy, but I'm telling you she could get around fine without a cane or walker or whatever. Purposeful movements, and always with this guilty side-to-side glance, as if she was afraid some insurance rep might jump out of the bushes and snap an incriminating photo, claim he'd caught her lifting heavy boxes, dancing a jig, running a marathon.

Joanne Huff was on disability of some kind. I always suspected she'd won an injury settlement against a previous employer: one of those deals where you figure out where the security cameras are, then find a slick, hard spot of floor to fall on. *Oh, my neck, my back, my ankle, oh, oh, get help, something popped in my brain.* Shawna would know the official story, at least, considering Stillbrook required background checks on housing applicants. There was probably information in the office files—depositions, medical forms, access regulations—but I didn't expect my curiosity would be satisfied anytime soon. Shawna never told anybody what was in those files.

After I unlocked the door and deadbolt on apartment F, I knocked lightly before entering.

Joanne sat in a puffy mustard-colored armchair, situated in the living room like the captain's command chair in whatever version of *Star Trek* you grew up watching. She had a TV nearly as big as the viewscreen on the Enterprise, though the sound was muted. "Good morning, Harris." Her voice was firm, but with a little quaver. I've used that same trick at previous jobs when I faked a sick call. "Shut the door. I don't want bugs getting in here."

I did as Joanne said, though I'd have preferred to leave it open behind me. She always made me uncomfortable. I think because I never really knew what was wrong with her. She looked mostly fine. Decent posture in the chair, all dressed in clean clothes, and her hair tucked under a terry-cloth cap, one of those weird fitted washcloths. One odd thing I noticed was that she wore two sweaters—a tan cardigan buttoned over a gray turtleneck—making her look a little bulkier. There might even have been a third sweater under the turtleneck.

She started doing that sideways glance thing, as if to make sure I hadn't brought someone else into her apartment with me. She made almost no physical effort to greet me. No attempt to swivel her chair in my direction, no turn of the head. If she lifted one hand in a feeble wave, I didn't notice.

Did it count as a disability if you *could* walk but didn't want to?

"Bathroom vent," I said. "Some kind of rattle?"

"Oh, don't worry about that. It must have fixed itself."

"Okay." I turned to leave, but then thought I heard the rattle myself. Funny thing was, the noise seemed to come from outside the room— maybe the apartment across the hall.

"Since you're here, do you mind…?" Again, Joanne barely moved, not even her lips as she spoke. Her eyes darted more to one side, downward slightly, indicating an end table beside her chair. I thought she was going to ask me to hand her the television remote, maybe even press the channel-change button for her. "My mailbox key. I'm expecting a package."

Probably her plan all along, but that kind of request wouldn't merit a slot on the maintenance list. I set my toolbox on the floor. "Just this once," I said, suppressing a sigh as I lifted the small key from her end table.

I don't know why I agreed, since it set a bad precedent. She could submit other fake repairs, and then, *Oh, while you're here, Harris, do you mind taking that trash bag to the dumpster? And could you turn the page on this magazine I'm reading?* I figured it was something to do with the stairs, since she managed to dress herself and cook and bathe, all without, as far as I knew, any nurse or friend or family member stopping by to help her.

So yeah, I took her key and clomped down to the entryway and unlocked her mailbox. The little compartment was full, but not with the normal junk mail and bills. Instead, there were two packages: one cardboard box and a padded envelope that the mail carrier had bent and rolled around the box before stuffing them both in. I wished I hadn't left my toolkit upstairs, since I could have used a couple of screwdrivers as pry bars, but eventually I tugged the box out, then managed to roll the envelope a little tighter so I could remove it without tearing the paper.

When the box shook, I heard the telltale rattle of pills in plastic bottles—room for about three of them in there. The box was hand-addressed on brown paper, rather than with computer labels and a pharmaceutical logo. I unrolled the envelope and gave it a quick inspection. No return address. The white envelope was that tough textured plastic, nearly impossible to open without scissors. The inside was padded, so presumably the contents were undamaged. I could feel a few shapes beneath the surface. More like lumps, but when I tried to pinch one it moved aside.

"Harris!"

"Got it." I clanged her mailbox shut, then locked it. As I headed up the stairs, I noticed an unpleasant odor, like rotten meat, but it dissipated before I got to Joanne's apartment.

"Two things," I said. I handed the packages to her, but she didn't lift her hands. Her eyes darted to the side, down slightly. I set the box and envelope on her end table. "Do you want me to open them for you?"

"I'll do it later."

"Oh. *Three* things, really." I stepped over to my toolbox and the envelope of Halloween flyers. "This is for you, too. From the office." I set one of the orange sheets on top of her packages, then turned to go.

"I don't like this at all."

I only had my back to her for a moment and hadn't heard the rustle of lifted paper. Somehow she'd managed to tilt her head and skim the flyer.

"Shouldn't think it'd make much difference to you."

"No," she said, "I much preferred the party. Kept the little poop stains from visiting. I don't buy candy, and I don't always have the energy to greet them at the door."

"Just one day a year, for the kids." I couldn't stop myself from making the point. Maybe it's because Shawna was so inflexible: no profit in arguing with the boss, so I saved all my wisdom for this strange hermit woman.

"They have enough days," she said. "Christmas. Birthdays. The whole damn summer."

"There's nothing like Halloween. Don't you remember?" I was prepared to paint the whole scene for her—like from a fifties black-and-white movie, with some splashes of pumpkin orange. Black cats in the shadows. Mist over a bright moon. The distant howl of a wolf. The rustle of dry leaves. Bare tree limbs stretched like skeleton arms. Kids with ghost and pirate and princess and witch costumes. Pillowcases stuffed with candy, and no dreams of a stomachache the following morning.

Then this thing happened to me. Maybe you've had the same experience. You know, how you're okay with something...snakes or bees, for example, or let's say a spider. Other people are scared of it, but you're fine.

There's one in the room with you, a blotch the size of a raisin, dangling at the end of a gossamer thread, and its weight pulling it down. You're wearing short sleeves, the spider's on target to drop onto your exposed arm, and you think, *God, if Mom were here she'd be screaming and jumping away, yelling "Kill it! Get it off me! Kill it!"* But you're perfectly okay. You watch that hairy raisin drop, and you'd even shrug if you could, but it's not worth the effort. The spider lands on you. It's not venomous, it's not gonna bite you. It's not crawling in some menacing way toward your open neck or burrowing beneath your clothes. It's just *there* on your arm. It's nothing.

You're proud of yourself for not reacting. Being so mature.

Then a violent shiver of revulsion hits you. Doesn't even need to be an obvious trigger. You haven't thought about the hairs on its vile body, the bristles along its eight unnatural legs, the click of those tiny mandibles or its predatory black eyes. It's just an overwhelming disgust, and you shudder and swipe the thing off your arm, and you want to dance and stomp your feet and make *bleh!* noises, tongue out and nose crinkled, and you're still scratching yourself a few minutes later, as if bugs had crawled all over you.

Maybe that kind of thing has happened to you? Once or twice? Well, I got this same sudden rush of revulsion about Joanne Huff. I'd been in the room with her awhile, not exactly *liking* her, but feeling okay about it. Doing my job. Being civil. You can't flick a person away like you could a spider, step on her like you could a cockroach. Then the idea of her illness struck me. Maybe the fact that I couldn't quite figure out what was wrong with her. When you don't know the disease, you also don't know how it *spreads*. I was standing there talking with her, more than I needed to, but could I get sick just from talking? Breathing the same foul air? Or would I have to touch her?

"Harris, what's come over you?"

I guess I couldn't hold back a shudder, but her shrill voice didn't help me calm down. There was a weird crackle in her speech, and it made me imagine the dry skin of her lips splitting. And then I remembered those kissing diseases like mono. You kiss the other person, put your lips over hers, press them together, mash them around, and the dry skin crackles, it's bristled like the legs of a spider, and a froth of contagious blood pops out, and your own dry mouth summons spittle into the mixture.

"I'm going to call the office," she said. I thought she meant to complain about my odd expression, but she was back on the trick-or-treat subject. "If I don't want kids coming by, I shouldn't have to tolerate it."

Her hand lifted from a crease in the chair, and she was holding a cell-phone. She probably had Shawna on speed-dial.

"No offense," she said to me, "but I loathe children. They knock on my door, and I'd probably want to kill them." She turned her attention to the phone, pressing a button with her thumb.

My signal to leave, which was fine by me.

"MY PAINTS are all messed up," Mattie said that evening. A simple observation, no accusation in his voice—almost like he didn't half realize I was in the room and might decide to punish the likely offender.

I pictured him saying the same phrases over and over while staring into the open tub of art supplies. "The red is in the white. The black is in the yellow."

Mattie turned around to explain. "All it takes is a drop. That's why you have to wash the brush when you change colors."

I leaned down to look over his shoulder into the open paint jars. The white jar looked like it was filled with Pepto-Bismol. The paint in the yellow jar had a nasty green-gray color, like something hocked into a napkin during flu season.

Mattie was careful with his paints—with everything, really. He was the kind of kid who didn't want different food items touching one another on the plate. "You think Amber borrowed your paints when she was working on that diorama with your mom?"

"The markers, too." Mattie pulled the top from a Crayola marker and waved its red tip close to my face. The felt tip was mashed down. "This one's new. I've hardly used it." He was wearing a T-shirt, his arms exposed, and he ran the marker's tip along the inside of his left forearm. Mattie pressed hard, a valley in his skin following the marker. He would have drawn a thick red line, the illusion of a knife cutting into soft flesh, but there wasn't any ink left. He ran the dry tip back and forth a few more times, making a sandpaper-scratch sound that really got on my nerves, and I had to tell him to stop.

"I guess Amber was in a hurry to finish that project for school," I said. "She's not as careful as you are. I'm sure she didn't mean to ruin your paints and stuff." I made it a point not to blame Amber too much, since I didn't want the kids fighting with each other again. "Your mom was with her, too," I added.

Mattie replaced the cap on the marker—though, of course, the damage was already done. It would never write again.

"Why don't you make a list? I'll get you some replacements from the Dollar Tree."

I thought that would make Mattie smile. He always liked things when they were fresh and new. Instead, he said: "She'll just do it again."

"No. I'll talk to Amber. Your mom and I will both talk to her."

Then I got another idea. I thought about when I was Mattie's age, how I had a secret in our backyard toolshed: a loose wall panel I could slide back, and I'd pulled out the fiberglass insulation to clear out a small compartment where I could hide comics and toys.

Well, there weren't any wall panels or other hiding places in our small apartment, but I could do the next best thing. Mattie's desk was a sturdy wooden junker Lynn and I found at a yard sale, and I'd sanded and stained it to make it nicer. The two side drawers were especially heavy, the bottom one deep enough to serve as a file drawer. "Hey, Mattie—how about I drill a few holes and install a lock on one of your desk drawers? That'll keep your stuff safe, won't it?"

And he sure smiled at that idea. For me, it was one of those moments where you're really happy to be a father—when you realize how easily you can connect with your kid and give him just what he wants.

From Digital Transcription #7

Interviewer: It seems to me that you're purposely misleading the investigators. Why would you of all people do that?

Victim: I'm telling you what I know. If you don't choose to believe it, that's your problem.

Interviewer: After what happened in your community, shouldn't you want the perpetrators brought to justice? I would think you'd have a special interest in seeing them caught.

Victim: You're still missing the point.

Interviewer: Why did you survive, when so many others didn't?

Victim: A lucky break, I guess.

Interviewer: "Luck" seems a bad choice of words. Do I need to show you those photographs again?

Victim: I'm well aware of how my neighbors died. My friends.

Interviewer: Why were you spared?

Victim: Okay. [Takes a deep breath.] It was something my wife did. She's a kind person. Always had a weak spot for children.

Interviewer: You keep mentioning children. It's impossible that children could do this. [Lays a photograph on the table.] And this. [Another photograph.] And this. [Another.]

Victim: I will never forget their eyes, those empty eyes behind their awful masks. [Pause.] We were spared because…[Inaudible.]

Interviewer: What? Please repeat your statement.

Victim: [Pause.] We gave them what they wanted.

LYNN

X

THE NEXT afternoon, I heard the pleading voice again.

A variation on it, at least.

I was taking one of my official breaks: fifteen minutes at ten-thirty and two-thirty, imposed by ComQues as part of their telework regulations.

I went into the kitchen to fix a healthy snack of baby carrots and hummus, and when I reached in the cabinet for a small plate, somebody tapped me on the shoulder.

I was alone in the apartment.

Because of our rigorous timed breaks, I knew the kids weren't back from school yet.

Their bus drops them off about three-ten, and it takes them five minutes more to walk home.

Not Harris, either.

Harris keeps pretty varied hours, depending on how many tasks he has, but I can always tell when he's in a room with me.

Part of the reason is that Harris makes a lot of noise, generally: loud unlocking of the door, clanking his tool chest on the floor, a loud sigh or two about how busy he's been.

But the other reason is that I can "sense" Harris whenever he's around.

It's another measure of how our marriage has changed, because it used to give me a happy feeling of togetherness.

Now his presence adds a kind of tension to a room. I always notice it.

So it wasn't my husband, wasn't the kids.

I spun around to see who or what had tapped my shoulder.

Nothing there.

Then I heard the voice again.

"Help me."

From the walls. "I need you. Help me."

I pressed my back against the counter so nobody could get behind me. The utensil drawer was to my right and I considered grabbing a sharp knife.

The voice drifted ghostly in the air itself.

"Hello?"

My scalp started to tingle, as if my hair was beginning to stand on end.

The voice said, "Is this the correct number?"

Then I sighed in relief and started to laugh.

"What's so funny?" the formerly sinister voice said.

All Harris's fault. Those damn ghost movies he makes me watch.

Once I heard the "correct number" comment, I realized what had happened.

My phone headset.

The old headset I had previously used had been attached to one of those curly stretch wires that connected it to the computer and phone line.

At break times, I would unplug the cord and drop the headset at my workstation.

But we got a new system last week, though, which is wireless.

It was much easier to use: I'd simply flip a switch to shut off the connection and I could walk around the apartment while still wearing the lightweight headset.

Except during this particular break, I'd forgotten to flip the switch.

I'd gone into the kitchen and a service call connected without my realizing it.

The click of the connection, then the unexpected weight of the head-set, had registered as a tap on my shoulder followed by ghostly fingers in my hair.

Nothing more than that.

Working as part of a computer-support call center, I'm used to hearing "help me" on a daily basis, from all kinds of people.

The same thing must have happened yesterday, when I heard a similar voice calling from the walls, from upstairs.

I've got to be more careful about turning off my headset during breaks.

And I guess I should be more assertive about what kinds of movies I like, rather than simply going along with Harris's choice.

You can help me with that, right?

But just because there was an easy explanation for what I had been hearing, that didn't mean I wasn't a little on edge.

Maybe with good reason, too.

THE NEXT day Amber shared something with me that bothered me enough that I started looking at this apartment complex with entirely new eyes.

Harris and Matt were in the laundry room in the connected building because we try not to assign chores based on traditional gender lines.

I was working on this stupid secret journal of mine and Amber was reading quietly in her room, but she came to ask me a question and I didn't hear her enter the living room.

Her little voice startled me when she asked right behind me: "Mommy, whatcha working on?"

"Mommy, what *are* you working on," I said, automatically correcting her grammar.

I didn't close the Word document, though.

Even a child recognizes the instant guilt of a quickly closed computer screen.

BRIAN JAMES FREEMAN AND NORMAN PRENTISS

She repeated, "Mommy, what are you working on? I haven't heard you talking to any of the people you help in a while."

"Oh, some days I guess people know what they're doing on their computers and don't need Mommy's help as often. They'll call eventually," I said, lying to my child as easily as any parent does.

I never realized until I had my own children how easily the lies could flow. Sometimes you just didn't have the time for the truth.

"Mommy, when you're done, could you help me type in my story?"

"Your story? You have a story?"

"Yes, and I don't want to forget it."

This was something new, and any new development with your child kind of wakes you up from the mental cruise control you're on.

A writer, eh? She wanted to be a writer. So young to pick such an educated profession! The pride I felt was very real.

"How about we type in your story right now?"

"If you're sure you have the time," she said. My little angel, always concerned about others over herself.

"For you, I always have the time. Let me log out for my lunch break."

I closed the window I was in and opened a new Word document. Amber came and stood next to my chair.

She said, "Okay, here's how it starts. A long time ago, there was a little boy who called himself Jack."

I typed: *Once upon a time, there was a little boy named Jack.*

"No, Mommy. It's not *my* story unless you write exactly what I say."

Well, I couldn't resist. I typed her exact words on the screen: *No, Mommy, it's not...*

Amber giggled and said, "Stop!" and then when I typed *Stop!* she said it again, louder, then we both got the giggles.

"Let's start over," Amber said.

"Okay." I pressed the delete key until the cursor had backed up and devoured all of the text, and then I gave her an expectant look. "I'll just type what you tell me. Nothing more."

"Promise?"

"Promise." I dangled my hands like spiders over the keyboard. "Now. What's your title?"

The Bad Place

by Amber Naylor

as Told to Mother

A long time ago, there was a little boy who called himself Jack. He lived in apartment 5D of the Stillbrook Apartments.

One Halloween, he started to feel very, very sick. He told his mommy and daddy that he was going to The Bad Place.

His parents asked him where The Bad Place was and he said he would show them.

It was Halloween night, but instead of trick-or-treating with his friends he took his parents to the basement of the other apartment building, where the laundry room and common area were. The lights were out in the big room, but candles on the floor made a bright star pattern.

Jack stabbed his mommy and his daddy with a big knife until they were bleeding out all of their blood. Jack didn't know he was doing this, a demon was making him do it.

When Jack realized what he had done, he stabbed himself and he died.

Halloween went on as planned because no one knew the family from apartment 5D was dead until the next day.

The End

I was shocked at the story, especially since Amber had set it in our apartment.

The idea that my little girl could have had such horrible thoughts in her head didn't feel real.

Yet I tried not to show too much concern in front of her because I didn't want to stifle her creativity.

I asked how she had come up with something so creative, and she told me she'd heard the story from those teenage kids who are always hanging around the courtyard.

They live in the other building.

So she *hadn't* come up with these horrible thoughts on her own. That made a lot more sense to me.

My Amber was creative and smart, and she wouldn't have dreamed up something so nasty on her own.

As the day went on, I found myself getting madder and madder the more I thought about what Amber had said and the horrible things those teenagers had told her.

What the hell had they been thinking?

They shouldn't have tried to frighten my little girl like that, and I'm thinking maybe I'll have to pay them a friendly visit to discuss their manners.

From Digital Transcription #7

Interviewer: Tell us more about Halloween night.

Victim: There wasn't supposed to *be* a Halloween night. Not officially, at least. October thirty-first was supposed to be just like any other day.

Interviewer: Did your community have problems in the past?

Victim: Not really. Of course, you hear all the stories on the news. Things that happen *other* places. Trick-or-treating simply invites mischief. It's not safe for the kids.

Interviewer: Who made the final decision?

Victim: It doesn't matter. Good intentions, you know? The whole idea was to protect our kids, which makes it pretty ironic.

Interviewer: How so?

Victim: It would have been a lot safer just to have a normal Halloween...

HARRIS X

"**A**RE YOU sure it isn't just that bird squawking?"

"I know what a bird sounds like, Harris."

My after-hours number was intended only for emergencies—a flooded bathroom or some bolt-struck tree limb crashing through a bedroom window—but Joanne Huff seemed to think it was okay to phone anytime with simple noise complaints. She was the reason I kept my work cell on vibrate after midnight and sometimes considered turning the damn thing off completely. I remember thinking: *If anything bad ever happens in the night and I don't hear about it, it will be her fault.*

"There's a county noise ordinance." I wasn't as loud and forceful as I wanted to be, since I didn't want to wake Lynn. "You're free to call the police."

She ignored my suggestion and continued. "Shawna told me there weren't any contractors in that unit. They shouldn't be doing construction work this time of night anyway—am I correct? Wait. Wait a minute. Listen."

I knew she was holding the phone in the air, turning it the way people do when trying to get more signal bars.

"I don't hear anything."

"Shhhh. Wait." After a moment, she gave up. "Well, of course it stops while I have you on the phone. But I know what I've been hearing. It's not any construction noise."

"Okay. What kind of noise is it?"

"I'd rather not say."

"If you don't tell me, then how am I supposed to help?"

Too late, I realized my mistake. I'd hoped to put her off until the morning, but now that I'd admitted the possibility that I might help, she'd never let me off the hook.

"Yes, good," Joanne said. "Only because you'll check that apartment now. You have to catch these things while they're going on. Otherwise I'd never say."

My wife shifted in the bed. Her back was to me, the way she usually slept. I moved my legs, trying not to jar the mattress as I prepared to stand.

Joanne said, "I'll tell you what it sounds like. It sounds like pleasure."

She paused, in case I'd ask her to elaborate. I declined.

"The wrong kind of pleasure," she finished.

AS I pulled some khakis over my pajamas and shrugged into a loose sweatshirt, I speculated on what Joanne might consider the "wrong kind" of pleasure. Was she homophobic? Or maybe she meant something involving animals or plush toys. Sharp metal points or leather straps.

Then I wondered how she would *know*. Joanne Huff didn't strike me as someone who'd ever experienced pleasure. This is a bit mean to say, especially since she and I were about the same age, but the best way I could describe her would be to say that she seemed kinda…dried up.

I didn't wake Lynn. She understood the hazards of my job and wouldn't worry if she found my side of the bed empty. I tiptoed to the hall closet and gathered my toolkit, so I'd look official walking around the complex so late at night. Also, I made sure I had my passkey and I grabbed my Maglite, since the electricity was likely turned off in the vacant apartment.

Plus, the three D-cells and metal casing made the flashlight a pretty hefty club if I needed a weapon.

Mostly I decided there was nothing going on. Just Joanne being her usual paranoid self. Somebody'd thrown shoes for a tumble in the basement dryer and the noise carried. Or maybe a stray cat or rodent found its way inside the vacant apartment. If there *was* a human noise in that apartment, though, I had a guess about the cause.

Stillbrook Apartments was within walking distance of a satellite campus to the University of Maryland, and college kids sometimes grew tired of their dorm rooms and went exploring. A few years back, another local apartment complex had trouble with kids breaking into an empty unit and having a "quiet" party there: beer, of course, and other mild drugs students might experiment with; whispers and laughter, likely accompanied with the usual late-night, dark-room activities. Nothing too messy to clean up after, at least initially. Such things tended to escalate.

The first group was cautious, enjoying how the forbidden location added fresh excitement to their partying routine. The next weekend brought extra recruits and the larger group became reckless: more noise, a few glasses breaking, some wilder physical couplings. And the following week brought even more students, trying to top the fun of the previous nights, not caring how rowdy they got in "their" secret party suite, until of course the cops showed up and the whole crowd rushed out at the sound of sirens—kids running in all directions, so many that the cops didn't know where to turn and caught none of them.

Following the usual course of rumor—that, and ratings-hungry TV channels—the whole thing practically grew into local legend. The kids had a few candles, since the apartments wouldn't have electricity. Rumor turned these into black candles, arranged in a Satan-suggestive pattern. And in all those furtive, dark fumblings, teenagers were bound to spill stuff. Alcohol, mostly, but some predictable bodily fluids, too. Rumor added blood to the mix—again, arranged in an ominous pattern.

Anything for ratings or to make the town seem more thrilling than it actually is.

So I was braced for college kids but expecting nothing more than a squeak mouse.

You know what I found, but I'll tell you anyway. You want this whole thing in my words, and that's what I'm giving you.

LYNN   X

HARRIS THINKS he's so quiet when he wakes up at night. I can hear only his side of the phone conversation, but the emergencies usually seem manufactured.

I've known for a while that one night I would follow him and see what he's really up to, but I didn't know when that night would come.

Does this make it sound like I don't trust my husband?

I guess it does.

I've always wondered what I might discover if I actually did follow him.

How about the night when I heard the ringing of a phone, some whispers about a bird squawking, then a county noise ordinance, then something about pleasure.

Since I'm writing about my problems with my husband, I guess I should be honest about the kind of things I'm afraid I might find out.

That night I was very still, listening to my husband's latest late-night call.

He moved to the edge of the bed, signaling he had decided he would be making another one of his unpaid middle-of-the-night emergency trips to somewhere in the complex.

He dressed in the dark and muttered to himself, "The wrong kind of pleasure? What the hell does that mean?"

I thought that was a *really* good question myself. What kind of stuff was he getting himself mixed up in anyway?

After that, I heard the front door of the apartment close as quietly as Harris can manage, which isn't very quiet at all.

Then I had a decision to make: Would I follow my husband or would I continue to trust him unconditionally?

If I didn't trust him, I could leap out of bed, throw on the bare minimum of clothes needed to be modest if someone spotted me, and then step over to our bedroom window to track where he was headed.

I might watch as Harris started across the courtyard below. He'd probably be moving slowly, half asleep, which would mean I wouldn't have to rush.

I could sneak out the front door of our apartment, just as he had, although I would close the door softer than he ever could. Wouldn't want to wake the children.

Once I was outside our apartment, I'd try to be as silent as a mouse in the hallway so none of the neighbors who happened to be night owls would hear me, but I'd probably run down the steps two at a time to make up for lost time.

When I reached the first floor, I would open the door to the courtyard and feel the brisk October air wash over my skin.

Then I would follow my husband into the darkness.

Yes, if I did decide to follow my husband, it would probably have gone something like that.

But what would I have found when I reached the other building?

Was he having an affair?

Or would I discover something far more horrible?

HARRIS   X

BUILDING SIX was what I call "Big Brother" to the one my family and I lived in. Stillbrook was made up of paired buildings, with one slightly larger because it had an extra half-floor to accommodate the laundry room and storage area that's shared by both buildings, with a meeting room that stretched out to the back. I started calling them Big Brother and Little Brother, since from a distance it's like the one building's a "head" taller, maybe putting its arm around the smaller guy like a brother. Shawna reluctantly adopted the terminology, since it's an easy way to refer to the building with the laundry and storage facility.

The laundry room might be more convenient if the two buildings were connected internally. As it was, since we apparently drew the short straw when we moved in, Lynn and I had to take turns lugging laundry out the front of our building, across the grass-split sidewalk, then through the neighboring doors, then down a half-stairway to the basement laundry closet. Struggling to unlock the door while still balancing the laundry baskets, I'd often hear the whoosh of a rinse cycle or the tink of dimes in a dryer—a likely indication the equipment was all in use and I'd have to abandon our stuff on the folding table to mark a place in line. A real pain.

As I investigated Joanne's complaint, this time of night offered rare silence from the laundry room. I waited next to the notice board in the entryway, listening for other possible sources of noise. Nary a squawk from the Durkinses' annoying bird, though I heard a faint snoring from behind their bolted door. I had a funny thought that maybe the bird had sleep apnea or something. Or maybe it could mimic those kinds of human sounds, too, as an additional way to humiliate owners. *Oh, I didn't fart, Father O'Malley. The bird made that raspberry sound. Urp. Oh, that one was me. Sorry.*

As I made my way toward the top floor, the stairwell lights flickered. I'd have to replace the bulbs soon, but it was always cheaper to make 'em last as long as possible. On the middle landing, I heard a frantic tapping from inside apartment C. That college gal likely pulling an all-nighter, clicking at some history or psych paper. Nothing from the Tammisimo place across the hall. I moved slow on the top steps, careful not to rattle my tool chest. If there was a secret party going on in the vacant apartment, I wanted the element of surprise.

I looked beneath Joanne Huff's door. The light was on in her apartment, which made sense, considering she'd just called me. But I also expected two little shadows for her feet, in case she pressed against the door with an eye to the peephole, checking up on me. That would mean getting up out of her chair, though, so maybe not. I waved a greeting at her door anyway, then held my finger to my lips in a silencing gesture, in case she considered barging into the hall to give me more instructions. Or ask me to take some trash downstairs for her.

I did a little cartoon-character tiptoe over to the vacant apartment. No light under that door—not even the flicker of a candle. I set down my tool chest, then held my ear as close to the door as possible without touching. Listening for the sound of pleasure, I guess.

I felt like I was living one of those horror-story moments where I was supposed to notice my nervous breaths, then a dull, rapid thumping, and, *Oh, God, it's my own heartbeat!* And, *Then I heard a scream of pure agony. I realized the scream was my own.*

Yeah, none of that happened. Nothing but the expected nighttime silence. So much racket during the day, I couldn't help but imagine I was poised on the edge of some disturbance: the rattle of heating pipes, a whistle of wind, the random snap of wood as an old building settles in its foundation. The buzz of a fly; the scurry of tiny feet along a baseboard, a banded tail dragging behind.

I fished out my passkey, then turned it inside the lock. I pushed the door inward, and the hinges didn't even creak. The vacant apartment would probably offer no significant surprises. I heard nothing; I'd find nothing. Still, I paused a moment before crossing the threshold.

I guess I'd had a premonition or something. This was where the worst of it began.

Opening that door.

LEAVING MY tool chest outside, I flipped the switch of the Maglite and cupped my left hand over the dish to control the strength of its beam. Enough light filtered in from the landing for the moment, and I followed my shadow into the vacant apartment.

With all my maintenance visits, I've seen every style of apartment in Stillbrook. There's basically three boxy floor plans. Normal one- and two-bedroom units, with mirror-image variations depending on whether they face the front or back, and a "deluxe" two-bedroom with den, which costs more because of the so-called extra room that essentially steals its space from the kitchen and bedroom closets.

As I stepped into the "extra" den, the door closed on its own behind me—not an ominous wind- or ghost-slam, just a regular close. 6E was a deluxe, like my family's unit in the attached building. Considering I've stumbled blind through my place plenty of times making a late-night pit stop, I could've found my way easily even without the flashlight. No furniture to bump into here, either, or kids' toys to trip over.

Empty apartments always look bigger, before they get crammed tight with years and years of accumulated junk. Three cardboard boxes sat beneath the side window, but otherwise the floor was clear. *Sure, sure, this place'll suit us fine,* I could remember saying a ways back, when Mattie and Amber were barely two and three years old. *It's cute,* Lynn said, and did a little spin in the spacious living room, not really envisioning a future where the same move might knock over a chair or crash a floor lamp into a TV screen.

I partially uncovered the flashlight and let the beam trace a path across the hardwood floor. The place smelled musty, tinged with a varnish or wet-paint odor. My shoes stuck to the floor slightly with each step as I headed to the back bedroom.

In the mirror floor plan, this would be mine and Lynn's bedroom—slightly bigger than the second bedroom, and with an attached bath. From the doorframe, I waved the full flashlight beam into the room, corner to corner, along each wall. No curtains, but standard Target-issue mini-blinds on the windows—closed tight, and with several layers of dust graying the cheap plastic. Hardwood floors here, as elsewhere, sticky again as I crossed to the accordion-door closet on the opposite wall.

The fake wood panel crackled when I touched it and seemed to push back against my palm. It was like putting my hand on an old witch-woman's leathery stomach, feeling her breathe. I wasn't sure where that thought came from, but it caused my first uneasy sensation of the night. Maybe I should have said I've seen enough, backed out quickly, and then insisted to Joanne that my thorough investigation revealed nothing.

Why worry about the closet? Ours barely held Lynn's clothes—it certainly wasn't big enough for a person to hide in.

But I put my left hand on the paneling again, felt the springy give-and-take of the accordion slats. I raised the Maglite like a club, then grabbed the door handle to give it a quick tug.

The door stuck. Those stupid plastic bearings always fell out of the metal runners, and you had to force them. I leaned into it, pulled harder, and the closet scraped open.

No need for the club. A hanger rod lay on the ground next to some disassembled shelving, but the closet was otherwise empty.

So stupid for me to get worked up. I decided to do a quick run-through of the other rooms and call it a night.

But that's when I realized I wasn't alone in the apartment.

Perhaps I sensed the presence before I heard it. My frozen breath fogged the air. A room's supposed to drop twenty degrees and that's when you realize you need to call a ghost hunter or exorcist. But of course it was the last week of October, with no heat turned on for this apartment.

The idea of a witch had already drifted into my mind, so it wasn't so much a laugh I heard as a cackle.

"Harris."

God, the breathy voice sounded like Joanne Huff. Like she'd finally left her lounge chair and followed me here. She walked so seldom on those spindly legs, which meant her movements would be slow and deliberate. Perfect for sneaking up on somebody.

I spun around, waving the flashlight's beam. The room was empty.

Another cackle. "Oh, Harris. Better do as I tell you. I could destroy you."

Clear as a bell but no sign of Joanne. This bedroom was at the far end of the apartment, too distant for Joanne's voice to carry through the walls. I examined the heating duct beneath the windows: Was it possible the sound had transmitted through the vents?

I knelt, then cocked my ear close to the duct. Dust webbed over the grill, and a dry stale odor wafted up but no sound.

"I could destroy this whole building if I wanted to."

Definitely not from the vents. An unnatural, wistful speculation colored her tone, almost as if I was reading her mind.

"Harris!"

Holy hell, that was the loudest yet. The weirdest thing happened next. A distant answering voice—*Got it!*—followed by a clang of metal. Then footsteps on the hallway stairs, getting closer and closer.

I rushed across the dark living room and into the den. I don't mind admitting I was pretty spooked, fully expecting to find the front door wide open, some grave-emptied ghost framed in the hallway, dragging Christmas Carol chains behind it.

Nothing there. The front door was closed, as I'd left it.

No more footsteps. But the voices continued.

"Two things. Do you want me to open them for you?"

"I'll do it later." Joanne, as I'd been hearing all along. The second voice was...

"Oh. *Three* things, really. This is for you, too. From the office."

Yeah, the second voice was mine. I was having a bizarre out-of-body experience. *Of course! I'd actually fallen down the steps and broken my neck earlier today, and was too stupid to realize I'd become a ghost. I've returned to the scene of my death, to relive the accident again and again for all eternity.*

Or, if I could rescue myself from the horror-movie atmosphere I'd spooked myself into, I'd figure out the more plausible scenario.

"I don't like this at all," Joanne said. Her voice came from behind me. The second bedroom.

The door was shut. A faint gray flicker appeared along the bottom of the door. I heard more of the familiar conversation as I reached for the knob.

More of the *taped* conversation.

Once I figured that piece out, the room didn't offer too much of a surprise. A folding chair and a card table with surveillance equipment on top. Two black-and-white monitors, a computer, and keypad. An unplugged set of headphones and small speakers. A dish antenna angled to pick up sounds from the next apartment. A power strip loaded with cords and another wire along the wall and out the window.

On the lit monitor, I saw Joanne's living room as if I was spying through her third-floor window. Our conversation played out and I noticed my on-screen posture shift as I tried to pull away from her. I remembered that weird moment of revulsion I had when I imagined kissing her dry lips.

Those perverse notions seemed inexplicable at the time, but a theory occurred to me. Some guy recorded her through the spy cam, listened to her voice, stared constantly at her frail, ever-still body. He wasn't attracted to her—nothing could ever get me to believe that desire was the reason behind his surveillance. But he'd be bored out of his mind, practically begging for some movement to relieve the tedium. That kind of attention, minute by minute, trying to catch her at something, anything—after a while, it would approximate *obsession*, wouldn't it?

Move, damn you. Be interesting.

And for a split second, the transmission shifted direction. In a strange alchemy of surveillance, I'd picked up some of that guy's twisted thoughts.

I turned down the speakers. On the monitor, my earlier self walked out of the frame, leaving Joanne alone in her apartment. For a lark, I moved the mouse arrow to the controls beneath the image, clicked on fast forward. Joanne stayed in her chair, barely shifting her posture. I held down the speed-up button a little longer, but got bored after a while and quit.

Well, I thought I'd pretty much solved the mystery. Joanne wasn't so paranoid after all, since there really was somebody using the vacant apartment. He made all the noises she'd heard: banging around in the bedroom at all hours, playing back recordings at high volumes.

Except you'd think somebody doing surveillance would be a little quieter at his job.

Why would somebody want to spy on Joanne, anyhow? She sure didn't seem the type to have a jealous ex-spouse checking up on her. The government wouldn't have profiled her as a likely terrorist threat: *Yeah, let's focus our efforts on frail stay-at-home ladies in cheap suburban apartments.* Best thing I could come up with was her mysterious source of income. Maybe an insurance company really was checking up on her.

I wondered what she was doing now. I clicked off the review button to bring the image up to date. Joanne sat in basically the same position. The only change was that she'd turned her head toward the window, where the hidden camera was placed. Her lips moved, but I'd turned the sound down and couldn't hear. I hoped she wasn't saying my name again.

Then I felt really stupid. A gooseneck lamp sat next to the keyboard, its cord plugged into the power strip beneath the table. I flipped a switch and the lamp came on bright as day. I'd been sneaking around in the dark, but the apartment actually had electricity the whole time.

With the brighter view, I noticed more items next to the table: an open carton of Diet Cokes, a grocery sack full of chips and beef jerky, and a plastic travel kit with toothbrush and disposable shaver. The guy obviously stayed there for long stretches—a fact confirmed by the rolled-out sleeping bag beneath the opposite wall.

He slept there? If so, I wondered why he wasn't there tonight.

Why hadn't he snuck up behind me to pistol-whip the back of my head?

That's when I heard a thump, followed by a heavy crash. I glanced at the computer speakers first, half forgetting that I'd turned the volume down. On the monitor, Joanne continued to stare from the screen.

The sound definitely came from within this apartment. There'd been a hollow, ceramic tone to the crash, which told me where to look.

"I know you're here," I said, stating the obvious. I stepped outside the bedroom, flipped the wall switch, and the ceiling light came on. Around the corner, the bathroom door was closed. "I'm coming in now. Just the maintenance man for the building." My plan was to calm the guy down a bit, make sure he knew I wasn't a police officer or something. That way, he'd be less likely to lash out with that hypothetical gun those surveillance guys always carried on TV.

I lowered the Maglite to a nonthreatening position, then reached for the doorknob. "Neighbor complained about the noise, is all." I turned the knob, pushed the door inward. No sudden movements—careful not to startle the guy.

Turns out I needn't have bothered. This guy wouldn't ever be startled again.

He was faceup in the bathtub, his clothes dark against the white porcelain. The guy had a medium build, though his cramped horizontal position made it hard for me to judge his height. Instead of lying lengthwise, his body lay stuffed into the middle—head beneath the soap dish on the wall, one leg tucked inside and bent beneath him, and the other hanging limp over the edge of the tub.

He had short straight hair and a Vandyke beard peppered with gray. A wadded piece of cloth filled his mouth; a rope hung around his neck.

When I turned on the bathroom light, I corrected my first impression. The rope was a stained blue-and-white necktie, with an amateur's looping knot cutting off his circulation. His face had a horrible bruised pallor, eyes bulged wide. The cloth in his mouth turned out to be his swollen tongue.

I've seen enough TV cop shows to know you're not supposed to touch a dead body. And who'd want to anyway, right? Sometimes they press two fingers against the neck to check for a pulse, but from his posture and expression, the guy was obviously dead.

My best guess: The other end of that tie had been knotted over the metal curtain rod. Over time the knot loosened, the dead body swung and shifted, the knot loosened further. Eventually the body fell with that loud crash I'd heard from the other room.

I'll tell you what it sounds like, Joanne had said. *It sounds like pleasure.*

The whole time she listened next door, Joanne heard his dangling feet kick against the tub like a workman's hammer. She heard a protracted gurgle from the strangled man's throat, trying to cry for help, because whatever happened—he'd been attacked, maybe, or tried to kill himself—in the horrible aftermath he'd fought for life, as we all would.

The wrong kind of pleasure.

No. I couldn't get my mind around that possibility. The man's trousers were closed, the belt fastened. His arms had fallen to his sides, hands twisted in agony rather than pleasure.

Yet I found the strangest thing next to him in the tub. A fresh wedge of lemon. It bothered me, why it was there, so bright and yellow and clean, next to that bruised, strangled corpse. It just seemed wrong.

Now, I can guess your gross little theory about that, but I don't think that's what happened here. Not at all.

Regardless, it bothered me, like I said. And there was nobody around to *ask* so late at night, and nobody I wanted to call, either—certainly not the police. Not yet. Not till I figured this out.

Before I go on, let me digress for a moment to say I'll never understand why people make such a fuss if someone doesn't call the cops right away. That's an honest reaction, okay, not a sign of guilt. I was in shock. I'd never seen anything like this, and it was taking me a long time to process.

Anyway, there was nobody around for me to ask except for, well... *him*. And, yeah, I knew he couldn't talk—I was in shock, not stupid—but I found myself looking in his face for some sign of what he *might* say, you know? Maybe the way you'd look at a dog and say, *Hey, what's bothering you, boy?* never really expecting an answer.

I stared into that face. That strangle-bloated face, with the swollen tongue. I looked too closely, and it's like one or both of us changed. I started out clinical, playing amateur sleuth or coroner; next thing you knew, I was a scared kid staring at a hideous corpse.

What bothered me most were the eyes. That's where you look when you're talking to somebody, usually, so I'd focused there without meaning to. They bulged out so horribly. Unblinking. Still surprised, still expressing agony or shame.

That's another cop show thing, isn't it? People close the eyes of a corpse—to respect the dead person's dignity maybe, or to make their faces appear less disturbing to the living.

Don't touch a corpse, except the eyelids are okay. Right? It seemed like the proper thing to do.

I spread my fore- and middle fingers in a wide V and stretched my right arm toward the dead man's face. I had to hover over the tub, lean down a bit to reach. As my fingertips grew close, a shiver of dread tensed through me. The face seemed too large, the eyes even larger, and I started to chicken out.

Dignity. Give the corpse its dignity.

I stretched my fingertips closer. But I felt too queasy. I turned my head away at the last second, gently laid my fingertips against the eyelids.

I pressed against the lids to lower them, but they wouldn't slide. The skin felt strangely firm and my fingertips couldn't get traction. I pressed harder. The eyelids were slick and springy to the touch.

Despite my queasiness, I had to look. I turned my head back toward the corpse's face.

My aim had slipped too low. My fingers pressed directly into the open, bulging eyes.

That was when I completely freaked out. I had to get out of there. I ran from that bathroom, crossed the dark empty living room and den, threw open the apartment door, and rushed into the hall.

Then I tripped over the tool chest I'd left outside the door, and my momentum carried me forward and I fell headfirst into the stairwell.

LYNN

'M SUPPOSED to be honest with you, right?

Can you be honest with me, Mr. Therapist?

If you can, ask yourself this: How far would you go to save your family?

What would you be willing to do?

What kind of horrible things?

If you stumbled upon your husband in a situation where he was in over his head, mixed up in some crazy mess, how far would you go to fix the problems he had made for your family?

Maybe no one knows the answers to those questions until they face them down in real life.

I certainly know my answers now.

A marriage will do that to you, if you're really committed to it.

Like most husbands, Harris creates a lot of messes for me to clean up. I don't have time to list them all.

But let me tell you what I do with our kids. Maybe you'll appreciate it, since Harris never seems to notice.

While he gets to roam around the complex all day doing his handyman stuff, I have to take tech support phone calls from our apartment, which means I can't leave.

In the morning, I make the kids their school lunches.

When my shift is over for the day, I drive the kids to after-school games, events, rehearsals, and any other time-killing stuff the school makes up.

The kids take sick days from school when they have the sniffles, but guess who takes care of them?

That's right, me. And I'm not even supposed to be taking care of them when I'm on duty for work, as I may have mentioned before.

When the kids need to go shopping, which parent is the chauffeur and banker?

Me again.

I play with them whenever they crave parental interaction instead of when a whim strikes me, as Harris does.

I know you told me I'd feel better writing all these things down. It's supposed to help, like an angry email to your boss that you write and never send.

But if you never send it, the boss will never LEARN.

You don't confront him, and your husband never learns to pick his dirty clothes up off the floor, for example.

I don't want to be the suffer-in-silence kind of wife.

Not after some of the messes I've had to clean up.

I'm going to have to take action to fix some of the problems that have developed around here.

EMAIL FROM
JESSICA SHEPARD

From: Jessica Shepard
To: Jacob Grant

J ACOB,

    Classes are a lot harder than I thought they'd be. I'm wondering if I made the right choice to move all the way out here. If I don't pass ALL of my classes, my parents will be PISSED.

    Also, have you ever considered how much fun it might be to kill a man?

Hugs and kisses,

Jess

HARRIS X

I LOST COUNT of how many steps my skull bonked against during my tumble to the second floor. Pretty sure I dozed off a bit, curled up next to a welcome mat and hugging my knees.

My head pounded. I dreamed of footsteps all around me, imagined a pound of raw steak dragged across a wooden cutting board. Someone placed a wedge of lemon into my mouth, squeezed it. The juice tasted bitter and coppery and rotten.

A series of phone numbers raced through my mind. Home. The leasing office. 911. I heard beeps as my fingertips pressed at buttons.

The buttons felt firm and wet. They burst, and my fingers pressed deep into jellied sockets.

More footsteps. A clock alarm, muffled behind a series of doors. The clatter of pipes, the distant hiss and spray of a shower nozzle. The hideous squawk of a pet bird.

I was a drunk passed out on a stranger's stoop, waking to the bustle of morning activity. I sat up where I'd landed, tried to shake off the throbbing headache. One side of my face was scuffed by the burlap "Go Away" welcome mat I'd used as a pillow, and my legs and shoulders ached.

When I stood, a bout of dizziness almost knocked me back to the floor. After a few unsteady steps, I managed to stumble down the stairs, past the apartment entryway, and then zombie-walked into the gray October dawn.

Body. I couldn't forget I'd discovered a dead body. The to-do list began to generate itself, an Excel sheet filling up with new, queasy responsibilities. In my mind I clicked in the top-priority cells, erased their contents, and typed in: Warm Bed. Comfortable Pillow. More Sleep.

LYNN'S ALARM woke me. I rarely heard it, since I was typically up and out of the house before she needed to get moving for her call-center job. The insistent beep exactly matched the pounding in my head, adding an electrical twinge I felt in my tooth fillings. I bit down in a grimace, actually chomping on my fingers.

Two fingers in my mouth. The same ones I'd touched the corpse with.

"Calling in sick today?"

My wife was cheery already, without the pre-coffee grumbles any normal person was typically prone to.

"No. Just need…" Instead of finishing the thought, I made spitting noises. My mouth tasted rancid.

"Matt's already awake, banging stuff in the kitchen. Your phone kept vibrating. Hope it's nothing important. Hey, you really don't look so good."

I didn't need a mirror to know she was right, since I felt dizzy again when I tried to sit up. I had this notion that if Lynn stopped talking, maybe the room would hold still.

"There's a cut on your cheek. How'd you manage that? I'll get you a Band-Aid, but I can't promise it won't have SpongeBob or Hello Kitty on it. Harris, you went on a call last night, didn't you?"

"It's nothing," I said. "Gimme a minute. Check'n see if your Amber's awake."

💀

AS SOON as I heard my wife in the kids' room, practically singing Amber awake, I checked the messages on my work cell. Four from Joanne Huff, exactly at the top of each hour. The most recent was from Shawna.

I deleted Joanne's, then pressed play for Shawna's. Her message was quick, delivered with false, customer-service sincerity: *Stop by the office first thing, would you, Harris?*

Judging from her tone, she hadn't yet learned about the mess in the supposedly vacant apartment. Her request seemed unnecessary, though. I was planning to visit the office anyway, as I did every weekday morning—but this time I wouldn't simply be picking up my spreadsheet of repair assignments. We'd need to consult about the situation in 6E. I had a pretty good idea how she'd want to handle it.

Of all her cautionary anecdotes about apartment management, her most detailed involved a horrible occurrence at the Stillbrook complex. Except nobody at Stillbrook knew it ever happened.

In 2004, a couple of years before I took the job and moved here with Lynn and the kids, a renter killed himself in his apartment. A middle-aged guy, he kept to himself most of the time. His application was fine: good credit history and salary; no criminal record or anything to indicate mental illness. Would never guess this guy would even *own* a shotgun, let alone be the type who'd jam the metal barrel in his mouth and pull the trigger with his right toe.

He'd only removed the shoe and sock from that one foot, Shawna told me. *I'll never forget that.*

It was a prime-time blast, right after people had finished their suppers and settled down for evening sitcoms. Everybody heard it.

Shawna wasn't on-site that late, but she got a few calls at home. Only one caller mentioned a gunshot. The others blamed kids and fireworks, or described a neighbor's car that must have backfired.

You see, we're a suburban community. People living in the same building or the one attached—they'd recognize it was a gunshot. Nothing else could be that loud and that close. But then they'd talk themselves out of it, since "such things couldn't happen here." I did everything I could to help them accept the more comforting interpretation.

Shawna explained how carefully she shielded Stillbrook residents from the police investigation, kept any whisper out of the rumor mill—because it was a short hop to press coverage, and then the whole complex would suffer.

A management nightmare. Who'd want to live in a place where something this terrible could happen? The director at Luxury Arms in Cleveland spoke about a double murder in a premium unit. Happened twenty years ago, and to this day he has to offer two months free and other signing incentives just to maintain eighty percent occupancy. That's why I scrubbed blood off the wall and floor and repainted the whole bedroom myself—couldn't trust the discretion of outside contractors. Don't dare mention this story to anyone, Harris. Not even your wife. Worst thing would be for this news to get out. For people to try to guess which unit was the site of this terrible tragedy.

A false note of mystery to end on, since the suicide obviously occurred in the apartment she no longer rented out. 6E, now the site of a second gruesome death for her to hide from residents.

LET ME digress again to say I'm telling you this because places have a history, okay? And that's important.

You don't need some ancient Indian burial ground beneath the ancestral mansion of a troubled family—because honestly, how much crazy psychic energy can a single family produce over the generations?

If a place is going to be haunted, it's more likely to be an apartment building, since there's a high turnaround in tenants, and folks from a variety of backgrounds will bring different quirks and neuroses and illnesses with them.

Going with the odds, an apartment building simply has more opportunities for crazy, haunted people to live there.

It's a decent theory, right?

Makes a hell of a lot more sense than blaming kids, if you ask me.

WHEN I got to the office, Shawna already had the day's spreadsheet printed out. She handed it to me before I had a chance to say anything. I barely glanced at the paper, trying to come up with an easy way to inform her of the current crisis.

A smiling *Guess what I found last night?* wasn't going to cut it.

"Proves I was right to cancel the Halloween party," Shawna said. "Some of our tenants are already pulling stupid pranks." She pointed to the sheet in my hand.

I stood behind one of her guest chairs, holding the back of it for support. "I'm afraid we've got more important things to worry about than…" I stopped as I read the first item, already checked off as completed. *Building 6, common hallway. Maintenance tools scattered on stairwell.*

"Our mutual friend Joanne Huff called that one in. I cleaned it up myself." Shawna reached beneath her desk and lifted my tool chest from the floor. She walked around and set it in the guest chair in front of me. She dropped it loudly to make a point. My tools were stacked in the wrong places. "Could have been a tripping hazard. You should store your things in one of the lock cages."

"Yeah, sorry about that." The second item on the list made me even more nervous. The location on that row was *unit 6E.* In the next column, the task description read: *Items for removal to storage.*

So Shawna already knew about the body. She put on a cool, business-like front, pretending this was an ordinary task—at least on her official document.

"Don't be surprised at what you find," she instructed me. "And make sure nobody else knows what you're up to."

Why *wouldn't* I be surprised? Perhaps Shawna knew I'd already seen the strangled "item."

From the beginning, her manner suggested we could only speak in code—a precaution to ensure this latest horrible occurrence would never become public. *Who'd want to live in a place where something this terrible could happen?*

"The items are all bagged and boxed up," she said. "I took care of that part for you."

The plural made my stomach lurch. *Items.* When Shawna stacked my tools in the kit, she made sure the hacksaw wasn't visible. She buried it on purpose, beneath the hammer and hand drill and screwdrivers. The blade would be scrubbed clean, but maybe a hint of gristle remained between sections of metal teeth after they'd ripped through skin and muscle and bone. *I took care of that part for you.* The body had already been in the bathtub, a convenient place for dismemberment. She hacked him into pieces, bagged and boxed them, then rinsed the blood down the drain. Shawna did the packaging and clean up; my half of the job would be disposal.

"I can trust you, right, Harris?" She stood close, without the desk between us, and as she smiled I noticed a red smear of lipstick across her front teeth. "This has to stay between us. You can't even tell your wife." Shawna moved closer, and I wanted to run out of there. Maybe back to bed, a long sleep, and I wouldn't come out from under the covers until this awful stuff had taken care of itself. I could pretend it never happened.

"A private investigator has been watching Joanne Huff. He's from her insurance company. They want to make sure she's getting the proper settlement."

She spoke in a little girl voice, as if she were flirting with me—and with that gruesome Bride of the Vampire smile.

"I gave him my full cooperation. The tenants wouldn't like to know that, but sometimes I have to let the interests of the *entire* community take precedence. You understand, Harris?" She stood within easy reach of the guest chair with my toolbox. I thought maybe if I didn't agree, she'd grab the hammer from the top and lunge at me, swinging.

"Sure," I said, but I took a subtle backward step.

"I let him use 6E. Gave him keys, turned on the electricity. He assured me he'd be discreet. I didn't want anybody to know he was there."

"Like a ghost," I said. My own little attempt at code, but Shawna didn't react to it.

"Not sure he found whatever proof he was looking for," she said, "but he's done now. We'll put his equipment in storage."

"His equipment?"

"Monitors and microphones and those little cameras. All that technical gadgetry. He's paying a weekly fee, and we'll store it for him. He said he might need to come back."

"Come back?"

"Well, he thought he might need to investigate further. He takes what he has to his bosses, they review the tapes—that kind of thing. Honestly, I'm sorry to lose him. He's been one of my least troublesome tenants."

"Until now," I said.

Her inappropriate laugh made my skin crawl. "He paid in advance for two months' storage," she said. "And he paid an extra month on the apartment, too."

She seemed so bloodthirsty then. The worst kind of femme fatale— delighted to cash a dead man's check. I needed to get past this ridiculous code—sorry to *lose* him—get a direct acknowledgment of what she really knew. "Shawna…did you, um, actually see him?" Meaning: Did you see the crumpled body? Did you see his pallid skin—his swollen tongue and bugged-out eyes?

"Yeah, I was just over there this morning. He paid me in cash, and I helped him box up his surveillance equipment."

From: Jessica Shepard
To: Jacob Grant

DID YOU get some crazy emails from me last night? If so, please just delete them. I think I got hacked or something. My mom called me this morning and I have no idea what the email to her said, she wouldn't even quote it!

I'm worried maybe something happened when I was downloading songs yesterday from a torrent site. I'm doing a full scan on my computer to make sure it's clean. Sorry if anything weird came your way!

Speaking of weird, I'm getting some creepy vibes from this place. Hard to explain. Sometimes I feel like someone is watching me.

Sorry, I'm in kind of a strange mood today. I'd better get to class. Sending lots of love to everyone back home!

—Jess

P.S. Did you know there are ten to twelve pints of blood in the human body? Makes me thirsty just thinking of it.

LYNN X

THERE ARE things you learn about your spouse after you're married that genuinely surprise you, but you probably already know that, don't you, Mr. Therapist.

I've written enough about Harris for now, but I should discuss what happened with those teenagers who were telling Amber that horrible story about the boy who murdered his family and who, for some reason, lived in our apartment.

I did like you suggested and slept on the idea of whether or not to talk to them.

In the end, my maternal instincts won out and I went to confront them.

I knew I wanted to be clear and concise when I explained why they had been jerks to tell Amber that story, and I fell back on my Introduction to Speech class from high school.

Who thought something you learned in high school would have a practical use in the real world?

What I could remember really did help me, though.

We had this one week in class where we had to convey a point in a persuasive manner without knowing how much time we would have to speak.

So the teacher, Mr. Garton, would be sitting in the back of the class with his clipboard and a stopwatch and he might yell "Time's up!" after thirty seconds or a minute or five minutes.

The class would then discuss whether you had convinced them of whatever your point was supposed to be.

The way we were given our topic was really different, too.

Mr. Garton wrote down topics on slips of paper and put them in a jar on his desk, and then we each selected one, so the process was fully random and you couldn't pick an easy topic you were already passionate about.

When it came my turn to pull a slip of paper out of the jar, I landed this beauty: *The "neighborhood play" in baseball is a travesty of justice the likes of which no self-respecting sport would ever allow.*

The words may as well have been written in another language.

I didn't hate baseball, but I didn't like it, either, and I certainly had no clue about a "neighborhood play."

I didn't even know what part of the game involved neighborhoods.

Was that a batting term? Something with the pitcher?

Or was it something to do with actual neighborhoods, like those old-timey stickball photos in the diner we loved down the street?

Luckily, this new thing called the Internet (or the Information Superhighway, as our teachers were still calling it then) filled me in on the major details and I was able to speak to the class like I knew what I was talking about.

This talk with the bad teenagers was going to be much easier because I didn't need to do any research.

I already knew my point: Scaring little kids is something only assholes do.

That said, I still put together a "persuasion list" of compelling reasons to agree with me.

These were compiled in order of importance in case I didn't get to make all of my points.

Use your big guns first is how Mr. Garton put it.

Once I had my "persuasion list" ready, I started composing my speech in my head, and when I had worked through my entire "speech" several times, I went looking for the teenagers.

I found them where I expected them, down in the common room of their building, next to where the storage units are.

Sunlight streamed in through the dirty windows at the top of the room, which was the sole purpose for those windows. Only someone ten feet tall could actually see out of them.

The teens were playing a card game of some kind at the beat-up table in the corner.

Music was blaring from one of their phones like a little boom box.

Music like that makes it hard for me to even hear my own thoughts in my head.

I shouldn't be afraid to name names here, but in case someone else is reading this, I'll just call them by some nicknames I made up on the fly.

I approached the four teenagers playing cards and I cleared my throat.

They couldn't hear me over the music, so I did it again, even louder, which sent me into a coughing fit.

The teenagers turned their attention to me, and their leader, who I'll call Tall Asshole #1, spoke.

"Hey, what's up, Mrs. Naylor?" he asked as he laid a card down on the table.

All of his friends groaned, and I wish I knew the game so I'd know if it was about the card or about me interrupting their game.

I had been ready to launch into my speech, but Tall Asshole #1 knew my name, which caught me off guard since we've never been formally introduced.

"Excuse me?" I asked.

For the longest time, I've felt anonymous in this apartment complex, but now I'm starting to feel like everyone has been watching me.

"I asked what's up?" Tall Asshole #1 said again.

"I'll tell you what's up," I said, trying to get back on the script I had prepared in my head. "You shouldn't be making up scary stories to scare little girls."

"What?" Tall Asshole #2 asked, faking that he was genuinely puzzled.

"Don't play coy with me. And turn that shit music down!"

The words were out of my mouth before I even knew what I was saying. I never swear in public, but that music was making my brain shake like the epicenter of an earthquake.

Short Asshole #1 leaned across the table and pushed a button on the screen of the phone, silencing the music. I instantly felt better.

"Thank you," I said, even though they should have done the polite thing and turned the music down when they realized I was there to speak with them.

"No problem, Mrs. Naylor," Short Asshole #1 mumbled.

"Mrs. Naylor, are you feeling okay?" Tall Asshole #1 asked.

"Yes, I'm fine. I'm here to tell you not to try to scare Amber again. I wouldn't look kindly upon that."

"Mrs. Naylor, I think you're confused," Short Asshole #2 said, speaking for the first time.

"Excuse me?"

"Mrs. Naylor," Tall Asshole #1 said, "Amber is the one who has been telling us the scariest, craziest stuff we've ever heard."

"Bullshit," I snapped, swearing for the second time and not even realizing I had used the bad word instead of the "safe" version, "bull-poop," which Harris and I had coined for accidental utterances around little ears at home.

I just couldn't believe that these awful teenagers would tell such vicious lies right to my face.

"Mrs. Naylor, he's telling you the truth," Short Asshole #1 said. "Amber makes up these stories. They're freaky and kind of amazing. She's super-talented. You should encourage her creativity."

"You will not tell me how to raise my daughter."

"Whoa, it's all cool, Mrs. Naylor. We're just making a suggestion. It's cool. Maybe you need to calm down. Your face is super-red."

I couldn't believe how far they would push these outrageous lies, you know?

He said my face was red, but I was literally seeing the color red before my eyes.

I've never been that angry in all my life, and I can't remember exactly what else was said before I stormed back upstairs, but I do know the last thing I said to them because it was high on my "persuasion list" I had prepared:

"Leave my little girl alone or I'll make you regret it for the rest of your short lives."

From: Jessica Shepard
To: Jacob Grant

HAVE YOU ever heard of the Halloween Children, Jacob?

They're everywhere around here. I can't seem to avoid them.

For Halloween this year, I bought a "sexy pirate" costume. I'm adding my own accessories to the costume, to make it unique and fun.

Do you think the Halloween Children will like me?

—Jess

HARRIS

X

RETURNING IN daylight should have made the building seem less ominous. The trip up the stairs was certainly smoother than my stumble down them last night. The typical sounds followed me along the way: the grind and slosh of a basement washer, the Durkinses' squawking bird, the breathy rasp of hallway heat ducts, the clack of typing from the college student's apartment.

But I knew what I'd seen in unit 6E last night and I dreaded what I'd find in there now.

Both doors on the top floor were shut, thankfully. From Joanne Huff's apartment, the *Hello, Maryland!* weatherman remarked that it would be unseasonably chilly on Halloween Day, *so your little witches and goblins will really need to bundle up for this year's trick-or-treating. Watch out for razor blades in their apples and check each chocolate bar for sewing needles, right, Meredith? That's right, Chuck. And make sure you supervise your children at all times. Be particularly cautious to avoid axe-wielding apartment managers, since we wouldn't want those little Buzz Lightyears and Princess Ariels to end up sliced and diced and tossed in different dumpsters all over town. It's real hard to find all the tiny pieces once they're scattered around like that. Now we'll turn it over to Jenn for her cooking segment.*

Well, with the mood I was in, and the aches and pains in my legs and shoulders—I wouldn't have been surprised if I really *did* hear that kind of crazy stuff coming from Joanne's television.

My head hurt most of all. Not simply physical pain but disorientation and unease. Is there such a thing as an emotional migraine? A spiritual concussion? I had something like that.

The door to apartment 6E was locked. I used my passkey once again for entry.

The mini-blinds were all closed, but those Target cheapies never did much to block sunlight. The living room was bright and empty, though not quite clean enough to showcase for potential tenants. Dust webs hung from the ceiling; deep scratches marred the hardwood floor.

In the corner sat the same cardboard boxes I'd noticed last night, when I'd assumed they were empty. They were sealed with packing tape. With black marker, Shawna had written A / V—for "audio/visual," which is less incriminating than "surveillance equipment." And *far* less incriminating than "internal organs" or "severed limbs."

As I looked at three boxes arranged against the wall, I realized they'd been lined up together so neatly, almost the exact length of a coffin.

I set my tool chest down, retrieved a box cutter from the open tray at the top.

Before I cut into one of them, I examined the sides to see if any liquid soaked through the cardboard. They all appeared to be dry. I tapped my foot against the left-most box, expecting a slosh from inside, but heard nothing. The way the internal padding reacted—Bubble Wrap or foam or wadded paper—it felt like my toe prodded gently against a person's stomach.

I clicked out the box cutter's blade, then positioned it over the taped seal. The blade slid easily through the tape. I had to be careful not to press down too hard, accidentally slicing into the contents.

Nothing inside stared back at me. I found a familiar computer monitor and a keyboard with its cord wrapped around it. Tiny speakers, more cords. I sliced open the other two boxes, finding the rest of the surveillance equipment I'd seen the previous night.

Nothing more.

Except for a long strip of cloth in the third box. A tie. Blue with thin white stripes. It was probably a spare. If it was the same tie that had strangled the insurance investigator, somebody had washed it to remove the stains.

I tucked the top flaps to reseal each of the boxes.

Turns out Shawna hadn't been speaking in code. Nothing sinister: just items to be placed into storage.

She must have made earlier arrangements with the investigator, though I couldn't figure out why she'd lied about the time of their last meeting.

It seemed likely she'd never checked inside the bathroom. She'd been so calm because she had no idea what had happened in this apartment.

The body would still be there.

Once again I approached the bathroom—the equivalent of the kids' bathroom in our apartment, opposite the bedroom my son and daughter shared. It struck me how the innocence of kids could be scooped out of a building, along with the furniture—intrusive equipment set up in the same place where they'd sleep or play with dolls or crayons, a lurid Peeping Tom violating their sanctuary. And just above the tub where they'd splash water, where Mattie would twist his hair into shampoo horns or Amber would cup a froth of perfumed bubbles in her hand, then blow it into the air—in a room with the exact same floor plan—some business-suited horror swayed from the curtain rod, fingers struggling beneath a knotted tie, feet kicking at the lip of the tub while a tongue-strangled gurgle sprayed spittle out the corner of his mouth. The knot finally broke, too late to save him, and the body tumbled into dry, hard porcelain, limbs splaying and snapping.

I reached to push open the bathroom door. My fingertips twitched at the memory of sliding down the jelly of wet, dead eyes.

The bathroom was empty. And clean.

I could almost think I'd imagined the whole thing. I'd seen something in the dark—an abandoned towel or bathrobe—and my overexcited mind filled it with a human shape.

Almost. But the clean was its own kind of proof, considering how the rest of the apartment had been allowed to accumulate dust and dirt. In her previous anecdote of covering up a death, Shawna proudly commented: *I scrubbed blood off the wall and floor and repainted the whole room myself— couldn't trust the discretion of outside contractors.*

I examined the bathtub. The white didn't exactly shine, but it bore scuff marks from a recent scrubbing. I knelt next to the tub, reached in, and lay my palm flat against the nonslip ridges on the bottom. The tub felt warm, from hot water washed over it again and again.

The idea was repulsive to me, but I leaned my head into the tub and took a deep breath, checking for the smell of death and bodily waste. The odor was mostly chemical, like wet paint. Another scent lingered, in the tub itself and in the whole room. A seasonal air freshener—something like Autumn Harvest or Pumpkin Spice.

In a small plastic trashcan under the sink, I noticed a wadded ball of toilet tissue. The paper was wrapped around something. No point being squeamish, considering what I'd already done these past few hours. I picked up the wadded white tissue and pulled apart the damp folds.

Inside, I found a wedge of lemon.

YOU PROBABLY think you know what goes on in a person's mind after an experience like this. A normal person's mind, you'd want to imply—to insult me, to show how my reaction doesn't measure up with anything rational.

Well, I can't tell you what's normal. Can only do my best to recall what thoughts occurred to *me,* in what order. Maybe you've got a list of stages you'll compare them against, like that anger-denial-bargaining-acceptance pattern for grief, right?

Obviously, I knew something awful had happened in that apartment. Suicide, I was thinking, but if I wanted to go full Sherlock I might wonder how he hadn't been able to save himself, the shower rod an easy distance from the rim of the tub, so he could have kept himself steady. More likely, somebody stood over him, pulled the tie tighter, kicked him back from the tub, taunted him in his final gasps. Who might that be: Shawna, after some under-the-table business deal went bust? How about Joanne Huff, the invalid afraid she'd lose her only source of income? Her atrophied muscles rippling with renewed, almost supernatural strength, she'd prove all the investigator's suspicions as she lifted him like a puppet, wrapped and knotted the cloth about his neck.

Or is it you *(turning to the gathering of suspects in the country-house drawing room), the college student from downstairs? You said you'd never met the man, but you slipped up earlier when you mentioned his name. Oh, don't bat your innocent eyes at me. The two of you were having an affair—and you learned he planned to return home to his wife. You punished him for his betrayal, didn't you? Didn't you?*

I could spin out scenarios like this all day. How about...some other resident found a surveillance camera pointed into her bedroom? Not that far-fetched of an idea, really. If he's already placed one set of spy cameras, how much trouble would it be to plant a few more? He could spy on the whole building, the whole damn complex.

Or maybe his death wasn't related to Stillbrook at all. A private investigator would have other clients, would have a history of exposed secrets that ruined countless other lives.

A lot of people would have wanted him dead. So, yeah, murder. Suspicion of foul play. Whatever you want to call it.

But I decided it was suicide, because that was the less troubling thing to believe. I wasn't an accomplice to murder, or obstructing justice or anything like that. Suicide is kind of a private decision. You can't arrest the guy who did it, so as far as I'm concerned, there's no crime.

Easier to look the other way. Play dumb.

All I did was move a few boxes into storage.

Honestly, once that suicide theory clicked into place for me, my conscience was clear. I didn't give the matter a second thought.

Though I will admit one thing puzzled me. If the guy really did kill himself, what drove him to it? Why would he commit suicide in this dreary empty apartment? And not with pills or a razor, or at least a sturdy rope, but with a cheap necktie he just happened to have with him. That makes the act seem improvised. Spontaneous.

As if something about the apartment drove him to kill himself. Places can have an effect on people. That's what all those haunted-house movies are about.

Or maybe he'd witnessed something awful on one of those monitor screens. Just doing his job, bored out of his mind watching this sickly, motionless woman. Then all of a sudden he sees it: something so disturbing that he can't stop thinking about it. The image undermines his sense of self, his sense of what's *right*. He doesn't want to exist in the same world as something that terrifying.

I wonder what that image might be.

Those computer files might be worth reviewing.

OUR BASEMENT storage rooms were pretty much first-come, first-served. Instead of assigning them to particular apartments—there weren't enough to go around—tenants had to wait and watch for somebody to move out, then try to be the first to latch a combination lock onto a freshly emptied storage cage.

You could see through the wire mesh of each four-foot-by-four-foot floor-to-ceiling cage. Not all of the cages were marked, so you didn't necessarily know whose stuff you were looking at. A lot of it hadn't been touched in ages. Stacks of out-of-date magazines and *Reader's Digest Condensed Books*. Old-fashioned televisions with rounded picture tubes: a phonograph player and some vinyl records. A Smith-Corona typewriter. A plastic bin overflowing with Barbie and Ken dolls swimming through a sea of tiny clothing. A lot of sealed boxes and beat-up suitcases.

Not much worth stealing, that's for sure. In better condition, a few things might pass as antiques, but really, you wonder why people bothered with locks.

Easier to use the garbage bins outside.

The tenants were on their own, but Shawna appropriated an "official" storage cage in each of the paired buildings. Her cage in building 6 was practically overflowing with party supplies, but my cage was full, too: all my tools, the stepladder and replacement bulbs; extra shelving and fixtures and extension cords; mop and bucket, broom and dustpan, and the cleaning liquids. Still, her instructions specified that I store the A/V boxes in *my* supply unit. I managed to stack the boxes in there okay, but I knew I'd have to move them around or scootch past them *every single time* I needed supplies for, you know, my *job*.

The idea irritated me a little. I wasn't thinking about the boxes as evidence, that she'd had me place them there to incriminate myself. Like I said earlier, I'd settled on the suicide theory, so I didn't dream I'd ever become a murder suspect.

Multiple murder, for that matter.

No, I was just angry about the inconvenience. And how typical it was for Shawna to make snap decisions, never thinking how much trouble she put me through.

So that explains the little spiteful thing I did.

That, and my annoyance about the canceled Halloween party.

Because I could see all the supplies in Shawna's locked storage area. Christmas lights and ornaments and the artificial tree for our "Holiday Party." Hearts and stupid Cupid cutouts for Valentine's Day. Balloons and welcome signs for our semi-annual open house.

And all the Halloween decorations that now, thanks to another of her snap decisions, wouldn't ever get used. Plastic pumpkins. Ghost and witch silhouettes. A hinged cardboard skeleton. Foam tombstones. Giant rubber bats and spiders, and spiderwebs made out of cotton.

Shawna usually made me retrieve the decorations before any Stillbrook event, so I knew the three-number combination. I dialed it in and un-latched her storage locker.

Thinking: Wouldn't it be cool if someone found these forbidden decorations and put them up all over Stillbrook?

LYNN   X

SOME MIGHT say I crossed a line by telling those teenagers to leave my little girl alone or I'd make them regret it for the rest of their short lives, but I don't think anyone who would say I crossed a line is a parent.

Sometimes, as a parent, you have to do unpleasant things to protect your family.

Things you never, ever could have imagined doing before you had kids.

When you start to suspect there's something wrong with the place where you live, where your FAMILY lives, you have to investigate that suspicion.

You can't ignore what your gut is telling you.

If some inner voice says someone is up to no good, then you need to find out what's going on.

If you have this nagging thought that there are people watching you when you go outside, well, you need to get to the bottom of that.

The sooner, the better.

If your family is in danger, you have to act.

Even if that danger comes from within.

Sometimes I think bad parents can be the biggest danger kids face.

We're supposed to mold them and prepare them for the real world, to make them into responsible little human beings.

So when Harris wants to show them scary movies, I wonder what exactly he's thinking.

Honest to God, here's what happened.

We help each other clean the bathroom once a month because it's a task neither of us will take sole responsibility for.

Usually, helping means retrieving a forgotten cleaner from under the kitchen sink and taking turns with the scrubbing and keeping each other company while we do a crappy job.

So one day I'm scrubbing the grout for what feels like the millionth time in my life and Harris is sitting on the toilet.

Not using the toilet, mind you, but sitting on the closed seat.

We always say to the kids, when the seat is down, the toilet is just another chair.

When you're all crammed into this small of a space, you end up with phrases like that, what can I say?

Anyway, Harris asks me, "What's the scariest thing you think these kids could handle?"

"What do you mean?"

"You know, if something scary happened, what's the scariest thing they could deal with?"

"Harris, I have no idea. What kind of scary things are you planning to happen to our kids?"

"Nothing to them, Lynn. I was just thinking maybe we need a horror-movie night to introduce them to some scary stuff. It really made a difference for me as a kid. Facing the bad things on the television screen prepares you for the bad things in the real world."

"The bad things in the real world? Like axe killers and people-devouring space blobs?"

"Lynn, you know what I mean."

Actually, I didn't know what he meant.

I also didn't know why he suddenly wanted to show our kids scary movies.

Sure, Halloween was coming up, but a scary movie isn't my idea of a family-bonding activity. I'll watch them with Harris now and then, but our kids aren't ready for that kind of thing.

Awhile later, after we had moved onto a more neutral topic, I started remembering how Harris and Matt had been whispering to each other in the dining room the day before.

Had that been about this so-called horror-movie night Harris wanted to have?

Or could it have been something else they were planning?

Do you understand what I mean now about how sometimes the danger comes from within the family?

I had a conversation with Amber about her brother one day that really got me thinking about how a family works together or pulls apart.

I was taking a break from my work and Amber was finishing up her homework.

Her brother was following his father to a repair job in one of the other buildings, so for the moment we were alone.

This is one of those conversations that I can play back in my head like it's on videotape.

I asked Amber, "You look up to your brother, don't you? Even though you don't always get along?"

She turned away from her homework and stared at the ceiling and thought for a moment as if she didn't know the right answer.

Then she looked me in the eyes and said, "We get along fine."

"Didn't you accuse him of breaking one of your toys last week?"

"It was a bad toy. I mean, not one of my favorites. It was an accident. Anybody could have done it."

She seemed like she was offering too many explanations. I didn't like the idea of her apologizing for her brother, either.

Since we were alone in the apartment, I said to her: "You can tell me everything. You know that, right?"

Amber laughed and smiled. "I don't have time to tell you *everything* we do."

"Oh, I know that. But if Matt ever did something wrong, you'd tell me, wouldn't you?"

Now Amber really focused on me with those big eyes of hers. Her homework was completely forgotten. She said, "Like what?"

I didn't want to give her examples and I couldn't be specific. That would be like leading the witness or putting awful ideas in a child's head.

So I just said, "I don't know. Maybe if he forced you to do something you didn't want to do."

"Like clean my half of the room?" she asked with a bigger smile.

"No. We'd *all* like you to do that."

She laughed again, but the smile kind of faded away. She said, "*Matt* can't make me do anything I don't *want* to do."

There was something about the way she said this, a kind of singsong rhythm like it was a line from a top-40 tune, and she tried to get the words just right.

Yet the emphasis was on the wrong beats:

MATT can't make her...as if someone else could?

And a weird stress on WANT, as if she'd actually want her brother to lead her into mischief.

Maybe I'm just reading too much into an innocent conversation, but the whole talk really got me thinking about what real dangers my little girl might be facing out there in the real world.

And what could I do to protect her?

HARRIS X

I**N THE** middle of all this craziness, Mattie asked me to explain Halloween. The conversation has stayed with me all this time. It's part of my connection with my kid: I can quote things he said to me the same way movie fans can quote lines from their favorite films. Sure, not everything out of the kid's mouth was gonna be as classic as *Use the Force* or *We're gonna need a bigger boat* or *We've traced the call…it's coming from inside the house.* But it was special because Mattie said it. His words were part of our time together.

If you're a parent, too, you understand.

Whatever I quote you about Mattie, it's gonna be one hundred and ten percent accurate. Better than a tape recording.

Now, *when* this particular conversation occurred, I can't be quite as certain. Times and dates don't always register with me. If I had to guess, obviously close to Halloween. I mentioned the decorations stored in the basement, so best guess would put it sometime after I'd found the hanged man in 6E…but not quite when Lynn found that nasty thing burning alive in our oven.

No, the oven thing definitely hadn't happened yet. Otherwise, I'm sure I wouldn't have made that wisecrack about traditional holiday meals.

"HUH. HALLOWEEN?"

"Yeah," Mattie said. "Who came up with the idea?"

We were in the kids' bedroom, but Amber was with her mom in the den. They were at the computer, working on something that involved a lot of Amber chatter, and I guess us guys needed a break for a while. I sat on Amber's bed and Mattie was at his little desk where he kept his schoolwork but also his paints and sketchpads.

"Halloween's always been around. Since I was a kid, but way, way before that, too. It's connected with the seasons—the autumn harvest, I think—but there's also a religious element."

"Religion?" Matt tested out the idea, found the combinations absurd. "Religion and ghosts and witches and monsters?"

"You're right, it does sound kinda messed up. I guess you're supposed to think of old guys in robes—like monks, but they were called druids then. And ceremonies, with a similar kind of order and ritual as a church service, chants or singing or whatever, but not really praying to God. At least, not as we understand Him today."

Well, I was doing the best I could—considering that I wasn't a Halloween scholar. Not then, at least. Most of what I knew then, I'd gathered from movies and from stories I'd read. Fiction, which throws in some facts now and then for flavor, but it's hard to tell which parts are historical truths.

"What about the costumes?"

I remember thinking how Mattie must drive his teachers crazy with all these questions. But he was so polite the way he asked, so I guessed they would forgive him. His eyes shone bright with curiosity and he scribbled over a sheet of paper with different colored markers. He was doodling, but that was his way of paying attention.

"Costumes. That all started with a big party, called a masquerade. Yeah, I think that happened back in medieval times, during the plague. This rich guy threw a party, and he wore a red robe and a skull mask."

Mattie switched to the red marker, drew a long hooded robe and colored it crimson. I kept quiet for a bit and watched him work. Instead of a skull mask, he used a black Sharpie under the hood, making a dark oval where the face should be. As a finishing touch, he took a pair of scissors and poked two holes in the shadowy face. The white space of the next page showed through, so it was like two bright eyes flashing in the dark. Pretty cool effect, and I told him so.

Getting back to our conversation, Matt asked me, "What about the candy?"

"That's what makes it fun for kids. More candy than you usually get during the year, and all different kinds. Hey, don't worry. We'll still have candy."

He wasn't getting upset. Or at least, he wasn't letting it show. He stopped coloring, though.

"I wish we were having our Halloween party this year," Mattie said. "I really liked all the decorations."

"Yeah, me, too." There I was, looking at this creative, cool kid, and all I could think was how he deserved the best. Everything I had as a kid, and more—again, the same way most parents feel. "Can you keep a secret?"

"Yeah. I've kept a *lot* of secrets."

So funny how he said that, like a little adult. As if some sixth-grader would have all these serious secrets. Life-and-death stuff, of course.

I looked to the door in case Amber was coming back to the room. "I know where the decorations are hidden." Next I described the basement storage area, making sure to stress that he should *never* go there by himself, and the decorations were all locked up behind iron bars, and not even an expert bank robber could get past the security systems Shawna put in place. I mentioned laser trip wires and alarm bells and strobe lights—maybe laying it on a little thick so he'd know I was exaggerating.

Then I changed the subject a little, telling stories about my childhood trick-or-treat days, how different things were back then. I also told him about the boarding school I attended in ninth grade, how sad I was not just to be away from home but separated from all the traditions I'd grown up with. For me, Halloween had been the worst of it—the first major holiday I'd spent away from my mom and dad and little sister. What saved me, then, was when I figured out a lot of the other kids felt the same way. Homesick. Halloween sick. We weren't allowed to have a party there, either. It was against school rules. We were supposed to be too grown-up for that kind of stuff.

This wasn't exactly a school for smart kids—though I didn't admit that part to Mattie, of course—but turns out we were a pretty resourceful bunch. One kid mentioned a haunted attraction he'd visited in Pennsylvania: a corn maze and hayride, with decorated setups along the trail. There was a fake cemetery, with guys dressed in sheets and moaning like ghosts. The hay wagon rolled past one area that was set up like a mad scientist's lab, with lights sparking and flashing and a green-skinned monster rising from the lab table. People hid in the trees with fishing rods, rubber bats tied to the ends, and they swung them over the wagon as it passed. The kid remembered a bonfire, too, and a stone altar with a person tied down, and men in dark robes chanting, one of them raising a dagger over the sacrifice. Another thing he remembered, too, was this large tree that kind of leaned over the path, one limb extending so it was almost like the wagon headed into a tunnel. And then a man's scream, and a body dropped from the tree limb, cloth over his head and a noose around his neck, legs kicking as the life was strangled out of him.

No. The more I think about it, I stopped myself before telling Mattie that last bit. I didn't mention anything about a hanged man.

What I did was, I brought the story back to our boarding school, and our section of the dormitory. We kids decided to turn our wing of the building into a kind of haunted attraction. We brought in leaves from outside and threw them on the hallway floor. We made tombstones out of cardboard, set up candles for atmospheric lighting, and cut out bat and spider shapes from construction paper "borrowed" from the art room. I remember I made my own zombie makeup out of flour and food coloring—and when the wet flour dried on my face and hands it cracked and itched, but I kept the mask on all night. The whole thing was a lot of work, and not near as good as the professional job they'd do at the fancy hayride. But it was fun, and it was *ours*.

That was the lesson of my story, which I made sure to highlight for Mattie. "You understand what I'm saying, Mattie? Life doesn't always hand you everything you want. Sometimes you have to make your own version of Halloween."

He nodded, and I could almost see gears turning in his little head. Mattie flipped his sketchpad to a new page, and I kept quiet to see what he'd do. He outlined a large square, then another one behind it—connecting the corners to make one of those 3-D boxes kids like to draw. Inside the box, he sketched in some smaller shapes, and after a while I could tell it was a room. When he drew a dotted line down the middle, I knew exactly which room he meant.

"Hey, that's *this* room, isn't it?" I pointed to the bed on his side, the bookshelf and dresser. Outlines of Amber's toys crowded the other half, including a small dollhouse and stuffed animals piled on her bed. "Now draw the desk, and yourself sitting there doing this exact same picture. I'll bet, if you had a really sharp pencil and a magnifying glass, you could put a small version of your picture inside the larger one, another little version of you drawing an even smaller picture, and the same picture inside that, and on and on. Infinite. Kinda fun if you think about it."

His marker stopped moving and his head tilted to one side as he tried to grasp the concept. I'd always thought that idea was cool when I was a kid, like when you face two mirrors together and the image turns into an endless tunnel. Kind of a magic spell, really.

"Dad?"

When I looked down, I saw he'd turned the page and started a different picture. An autumn tree, bare of leaves. He drew some orange pumpkins on the ground and was ready to make faces in them.

I guess I'd zoned out for a minute. "What'cha need, kid?"

"Does my Halloween have to have religious stuff in it?"

"Nah. I think you can just stay with the pumpkins and ghosts and monsters."

"Good. Because I understand how religion fits, the more I think about it, but I think Halloween is better without it. It's like the movie you let me borrow, and things get worse when the priest visits."

I'd forgotten I loaned that one to him. A little too disturbing for a sixth-grader—for *most* sixth-graders, I'd say—but I figured Mattie could handle it. "Keep that between us, okay? If your mom finds out I let you see it, her head would probably spin all the way around just like that girl in the film."

"I'm done with it. I can give it back. Turn around for a second and count to ten."

I played along. I heard him unlatch his paint set, lifting a compartment, and I could pretty much figure out where he'd hidden the key to his desk drawer.

"Okay, you can look now." He unlocked the drawer I'd fixed for him, then he took out the DVD and gave it to me. Out of respect for his privacy, I didn't peer into the drawer to see what else he had stashed in there.

"I hope it didn't give you nightmares," I said.

"No." Mattie locked the drawer again, then held the key in his fist. He'd wait until after I left the room to return the key to its hiding place. "It was a movie. It wasn't real."

From: Jessica Shepard
To: Jacob Grant

THE HALLOWEEN Children are watching me. They're watching us all, Jacob. Forget what I said about coming to visit. Don't come near this place. It's too late for me, but you can still save yourself.

PLEASE DO NOT COME HERE.

There is NO ESCAPE once you enter this place.

There was once a boy named Jack who stabbed his parents because a DEMON MADE HIM DO IT.

There once was a man who blew his brains out with a SHOTGUN.

He PULLED THE TRIGGER with his BIG TOE.

What if that man is still here?

A shotgun blows off half of your face and where does it go?

IT SEEPS INTO THE WALLS.

He's here NOW, Jacob.

I researched photos of gunshot wounds. I found one that I think was taken in my apartment.

HIS FACE IS IN THE WOOD PANELING IN THE BACKGROUND.

PLEASE DO NOT COME HERE.

—Jess

<<attachment: gunshot-wound33.jpg>>

LYNN   X

HAVE I told you about how the kids started pulling away from Harris
and me?

There were little signs at first, but I'm their mother and I noticed
right away.

They had started to keep secrets from us, for one thing.

Harris thought this was no big deal.

Sometimes I really wonder about the man I married.

Secrets lead to lies.

Lies lead to trouble.

All kinds of trouble.

For example, you would think I'd be happy when Amber and Matt
started spending more time in their room without fighting, but somehow
the change in behavior was troubling to me.

I tried to talk to Harris about it while doing the dishes one night
after dinner.

"What do you mean?" he asked.

"Isn't it strange that they're suddenly spending so much time in their
room, especially in the evening when we're supposed to be having family time?"

"Well, we were supposed to have the scary movie night together, but you vetoed that idea. Besides, they're getting older and learning how to be a real brother and sister. Give them their privacy."

"Kids need supervision, Harris."

"They're kids, Lynn. For God's sake, it's perfectly normal."

"I don't like it. They're being too secretive."

"And you're being too snoopy. And kind of crazy."

That was a little uncalled for, don't you think?

"We keep secrets from them," he continued. "Why shouldn't they get the same courtesy?"

"Adult secrets are different. Children keep secrets about the wrong things."

"Oh, their lives aren't as complex as you'd like to think. Like when a kid laughs and won't tell you what's funny? Maybe they're laughing at their parents or their teachers, making a mean comment at a classmate's expense, but nine times out of ten it's some harmless poop joke. It's not like they're whispering government secrets or planning to take over the world. Kids can be mischievous, but they're not sinister."

Deep down, I was pretty sure Harris really believed that kids couldn't be complex.

At least about most kids, especially our kids.

I had my doubts.

Not about Amber, of course, but about Matt.

Perhaps my biggest fear, if I'm being totally honest, was that Matt would influence his sister in some terrible way.

That Matt would get Amber to lie for him, maybe, and that lie would hurt the whole family.

Harris and I didn't finish the conversation because it was clearly becoming a fight, which we tried to avoid, but that night, after Harris fell asleep, I decided I would be a bad parent if I didn't do *something* to find out what our kids were doing.

Asking the kids wouldn't get me to the truth since kids are amazing liars, and Harris thought I was acting crazy (his words), so I might need to get creative.

The more I thought, the more clear the idea become.
Something would have to be done.
But what?

HARRIS

"WHAT ABOUT your big secret with Amber? The book you two are working on."

It was my wife's turn to do the kids' laundry, but I was helping her fold. We let the clothes stack between us on the living room couch, cross-hatching the items to separate Amber's stuff from Matt's.

"All Amber's story," she said. "I'm only writing it down."

"Why keep it a secret, then? Since secrets are supposed to be so dangerous and all, according to you." I admit that I mocked Lynn's earlier concerns, mostly to distract her uncanny intuition away from what was really bugging me. *Oh, nothing. Found a hanging corpse next door, is all.* I didn't want to talk about it.

"Don't be ridiculous," she said. "Amber's not ready to share the story until it's finished. Simple as that. A lot of authors feel the same way."

"Now she's an author, huh." We set the piles of folded shirts on the coffee table, then dumped out the socks from the other basket. I took a break for a bit, since I never liked matching up the socks, but Lynn didn't seem to mind. "You could still tell me what it's about. She didn't make you sign a confidentiality agreement, did she?"

"Oh, you wouldn't understand it," Lynn said. "The subject matter's completely beyond you. It's a love story."

"Very funny. Matter of fact, I already learned from Matt that it's a Halloween story. Unless it's a love story, too? 'Cupid's Skeleton'? 'Romancing the Pumpkin'? Am I getting close?"

"Miles away." She matched a few more socks, and I helped with the stragglers. All the while, I tried to think of the silly things little Amber might come up with. She had a cute way of thinking, putting ideas together that didn't quite fit. Not as logical as Mattie, so sometimes she'd surprise you. Years ago at the zoo, she described an elephant as a big gray toad. She explained by pointing at the sign, which she couldn't actually read. *See? It says epi-toad.* Of course, I always reminded her during *Dumbo* or during the "epitoad" stampede of a Tarzan flick. Lynn got a little mad that I wouldn't let stuff like this go, but Amber just laughed. *I never said that, Daddy.*

A series of thumps pulled me out of my reverie. At first I thought it was Amber or Matt running behind the couch, but then I realized it was the upstairs guy again—Mr. Stompy. He crossed from one end of his apartment to the other, then back again. If we had a chandelier in our living room, its crystal pendants would have jangled with each stomp.

"Jeez, sounds like he weighs four hundred pounds."

"He's a nice old man," Lynn told me. "Frail old thing."

"Then he must be doing it on purpose." Since he was a recent move-in, I'd barely met him myself—he never called for any repairs, I'll give him credit for that—but this constant inconsiderate movement was ridiculous. "Why couldn't we have gotten Joanne Huff as our upstairs neighbor? She never gets out of her chair, so she'd be pretty quiet." Another stomping pass across the room. "I'd like to cut off his feet."

"I wish you wouldn't say things like that."

The expression on Lynn's face—a mix of paranoia and disappointment—made me think her intuition had seen through me after all. She sensed my gruesome discovery of the night before, divined my nightmare speculations of Shawna using my handsaw to grind, businesslike, through the corpse's bones.

Lynn knew it all. Couples can read each other's minds like this sometimes. And she was thinking how awful it was for me, at a time like this, to joke—yes, Lynn at least knew I was joking—about cutting off a man's feet.

"What?" I said, playing innocent. Those things never happened. I'd decided never to speak of them.

In answer, she offered a quick tilt of her head toward the kids' bedroom. I almost sighed with relief. My wife didn't have a witch's intuition after all, and was simply revisiting a tiresome argument. Little pitchers have big ears, if I'm quoting right. The idea that, when we think they aren't listening, or even aren't in the same room, our kids might hear what we say—or misconstrue a vague tone in our voice—and somehow Mattie or Amber would then be influenced in some hypothetical, negative way. Always watch what you say, how you say it. *I* know you're joking, Harris, but they might not. Like it or not, you're a role model. They admire you.

For this reason, Lynn might wince whenever I complained about our neighbors. What a nuisance they were. How the world would be better off without them. Some of them. Most. Sure, the kids might have heard me say stuff like this now and again. It shouldn't have done any harm, and I never liked Lynn to make such a big deal about it. Especially when the joke was between us, and the kids weren't anywhere around.

"Us two." I waved a forefinger back and forth between us, reminding her the kids weren't around, that we're allowed to have a different language when we're alone, that parents need an occasional sanctuary from obsessive concerns about two preteen children. Moments of privacy. Secrets. Which brought us full circle to the start of the discussion, which I'd now won decisively.

Though I didn't say all that. Just "Us two" and the finger gesture.

Lynn wrinkled up her nose in a universal symbol of distaste, clearly directed at "my attitude," and I braced myself for a shrieking, severe restatement of her argument.

Instead, she said, "Do you smell something burning?"

Lynn didn't wait for my response. She jumped up from the living room couch and headed toward our kitchen. I followed behind, knocking over a neat stack of socks in the process.

My wife went straight for the stove. Nothing on top, but black smoke clouding from the oven and the smell of burnt cloth and singed hair. She flung open the oven door and the odor intensified, but something worse accompanied the smell. A muffled cry. A kind of animal sound but hauntingly familiar.

Because it wasn't an animal. Although hard to decipher, these were human sounds, a choked gagging attempt at speech.

Lynn yelped like she'd been burned. Her body blocked my view, so I couldn't see into the oven. She reached for insulated mitts, folding them over instead of taking time to place her hands in, then quickly pulled out the baking tray. She dropped it with a clatter on the stovetop.

The creature was still alive. It wriggled against binding cords of twine, tried to roll its body or twist its head where it had burnt and fused to the metal tray. There was a small gag tied around its mouth, and it screamed through the cloth, an awful vocabulary of anguish.

And then Lynn was screaming, too. Telling me to do something, do something *now*.

But I was paralyzed. I couldn't make any sense out of what was happening. A little man, bound and gagged, placed on a cookie tray and baked in our oven. He was an impossible size, about a foot long where he lay, and wore a little doll suit of clothes to match. The clothes were burnt, his skin an odd texture of white and pink and golden brown. His body buckled on the tray, and it clattered against the stovetop. Lynn kept screaming, and I know she was telling me to put him out of his misery, telling me to kill him, but I wanted her to be quiet so I could hear the little man. What was he saying? What did *he* want me to do?

Sentences. He was trying to form sentences—that regular beat of words in human speech, but the words were too muffled and foreign for me to understand.

Perhaps if I untied the gag. If I reached with delicate fingers and pulled at the tiny knot in the tiny strip of cloth.

Now, Harris, now. And Lynn had given me a cast-iron frying pan and she was making chopping motions in the air with her hand and pointing at the strange little man. *Do it now. Hurry, I can't stand it, hurry before—*

"What's going on?"

Mattie's voice, full of curiosity. He was standing at the entry to the kitchen, unsure if he should enter.

Lynn's face filled with horror. She told him not to come in, said there are some things a child shouldn't ever see, ever, and then another twist in her face and I knew Amber was behind our son, peering over his shoulder, ready to push them both into the room.

Lynn hated me in that moment, my weakness, and she reached for the frying pan, but my own parental instinct finally kicked in and I shrugged her off, raised the pan, and brought it down hard on the gagged, screaming head.

I hit it so hard, I ended up knocking the tray off the stove. A spray of blood went up, the tray flipped over, then over again, landing straight up on the kitchen floor.

As the horrible, uncanny thing lay dead there, all of us watching in stunned silence, I realized it wasn't a little man after all—though it had been dressed like one. In quiet stillness, even with the disguise of the costume and the horrible crisping of its features, I finally understood what I was looking at. The burnt diagonal strip of black cloth over one eye, like a pirate's eye patch. And the gag, not covering a human mouth but a beaked one that can mimic human sounds.

I don't know why I said this out loud, and it took me awhile to convince Lynn I wasn't making light of what had happened. But as we stared aghast at that poor dead animal, as Amber asked, "What is it, Daddy?"—all I could think of was another of Amber's silly childhood names for things, a mistake she'd uttered at a pet store when she was five years old, making the girl behind the counter laugh.

What is it, Amber? I'll tell you.

"Para-tweet," I said.

LYNN X

OUR KIDS did something terrible.

Or, let's be realistic, Matt did a terrible thing and got poor Amber to cover for him. That's the only possible explanation.

He drew his sister into some kind of sick joke.

How awful Amber must have felt, seeing how it played out.

As much as the sounds, the smoke, and the smell bothered me, imagine how they made poor Amber feel?

If she felt responsible in any way, that makes it even worse for her.

Will she see the smoke, even when she closes her eyes to try to sleep?

Will she smell the cooked flesh and feathers?

Will the bird cry out to her tonight in her dreams?

All I can think is, *What will happen next?* Left alone, this kind of thing surely won't be an isolated incident.

So we can't leave it alone.

Harris and I, we have to put aside our differences and create a united front. We have to be effective parents.

Both of us, for once.

Nothing like this can ever happen again.

Jesus, that poor bird.

HARR|S   Χ

"HE WAS wearing a little pirate costume."

Mattie spoke as if making a simple observation. No shock of horror at the bird's corpse, or the way that small costume cooked and fused to its burnt feathers. I knew Lynn would hold that against him, that he didn't cry and carry on the way Amber did at the sight of the neighbors' exotic bird pulled from our smoking oven.

When we were alone, I expected my wife would tell me about serial killers and their early training with animals. The fact that this particular tortured animal had been dressed as a little man would add weight to her argument. I mentally prepared my counter argument: *Serial killers start with spider legs and fly wings, then go on to stray kittens and puppies. There's no birds in between. Everybody knows that.*

You think I'm making light of what happened later? No. I'm simply telling you how the situation struck me at the time—and humor, of course, is how some people react during a crisis. Dark humor, in my case. And remember, we're only talking about a bird. Sure, the thing might mimic words in our language, but that didn't make it one of us. I'll admit to being creeped out when I heard those muffled syllables, thinking it was a man's voice screaming for help, let me out, I'm burning

---

up, oh God, I'm burning up. In actuality, the gagged bird was attempting its usual sounds, discovering meaningless phrases. Pretty lady. Polly wants a cracker.

I mean, it was a nasty and horrible prank, don't get me wrong. Terrible way for that bird to die. But is it any worse than dropping a lobster into a pot? I'd made no secret of my dislike for the bird and wasn't sorry I'd never again have to hear that annoying squawk. So sure, let's suppose for a moment that Mattie really did cook the neighbor's bird in our oven—and I don't believe for a minute that he did. I still found it pretty hard to get worked up about the so-called crime.

Lynn was the exact opposite. She was determined to identify the culprit, learn the truth about what happened.

She had a *plan*.

First thing she did was put the kids in separate rooms so they couldn't influence each other's stories. Classic divide and conquer. She shut Mattie in the kids' room and Amber in our bedroom, then she strategized with me in the kitchen. Lynn was thinking aloud at first, almost muttering as she moved aside some Seen-on-TV gimmick appliances to get at the larger food containers in our cabinets. One phrase I remember was "Can't believe you said 'Para-tweet,'" but I knew better than to engage in conversation at this point. She sized the containers over the dead bird, imagining some respectful delivery in a Tupperware coffin. Smoke still lingered in the room, along with the smell of burnt feathers and seared meat. I coughed for a minute, then switched on the blower over the stove.

"We should take it out of the costume. Oh Harris, find me a spatula, would you? This poor thing is stuck to the tray. God, our kids. Our *kids*. You'll have to take it to Todd and Marie. I can't bear to face them."

The whole time, I'm thinking a small garbage bag would suffice. The Durkinses don't need to see this. Much better for them to think birdie just flew away.

"Scratch that, Harris. Mattie or Amber should take it to them. That can be part of their consequence."

She actually said "consequence" instead of "punishment." That's language from parent-teacher conferences, not the kind of thing you'd hear in a regular home like ours.

"It's best that you be strict with Amber, and I'll take the firmer approach with Mattie. We might have to threaten them if they don't tell the truth. Turn them against each other if we have to." As she outlined her strategy, she placed a bed of Bounty towels in an oblong Tupperware container, then lay the spatula-scraped bird on top. "We can't waver on this. Don't you dare undermine me, Harris."

I wouldn't dream of it, and I told her so, the vent rattling over the stove, the bird ungarnished in its plastic sarcophagus. The animal's muffled cries still lingered in my memory, an unsettling mix of human and mechanical speech, like the voice of a robot suddenly discovering it could feel pain.

"God, where's the lid for this one, Harris? Where's the damn lid?"

LYNN'S STRATEGY wasn't terribly effective during the interrogation of Mattie. We stood in the den, two adults towering over the kid, and he wasn't giving the reactions she expected. Almost no reactions at all, other than a puzzled, quizzical expression. No remorse, certainly.

Which made sense if he hadn't done anything. An innocent boy would be puzzled by his kind mother's serious, stern questions—almost as if she'd transformed into a different person. He wouldn't know what she'd want him to say. He'd stay calm, infuriating her further, and she'd sigh and rephrase her questions, her voice louder with each new iteration.

"I didn't do it, Mom." He looked at her with wide eyes, then at me. "I didn't do anything."

Of course, a prejudiced observer could read these calm statements differently. He acts *too* innocent. His statements don't vary, as if they've been memorized. This is a game to him. The child acts this way because he knows exactly how to frustrate his interrogator.

The worst possibility, and I think what Lynn feared all along: Mattie was so calm, not simply because he didn't feel guilt, but because he didn't feel anything. He'd killed a living creature, and it didn't bother him. Our son had no soul. He was a monster.

That fear pushed Lynn further. She scowled at him, said she didn't believe him, said things would go rough if he didn't admit the truth. "We'll talk to Amber, too. Your sister will tell us what really happened. And if she doesn't, we'll just have to punish you both."

"I didn't," Mattie said. "You know I didn't." But he was a bit scared now. Scared at the threat, of course, but maybe scared of his mom, too. It's like his guard fell down. It seemed like he was nearly ready to confess—whether he was guilty or not.

I had a vivid memory from my own childhood. My father accused me of…well, I don't remember exactly, and it's not important. Say a window or flowerpot got broken, some money went missing, my sister fell and cried and said I pushed her. Doesn't matter. What I remember is how angry my father got, and how he wouldn't listen when I said I was innocent. He pointed to a wooden paddle he'd made in the garage, then hung on a nail in our living room wall. He'd written "Board of Education" on the thick piece of wood—a mean-spirited pun, I guess, though I hadn't understood it at the time. I said again I didn't do it, actually yelled at him because he wouldn't listen, and he said *That's it* and reached for the paddle. Afterward, I noticed splinters in my hands. Didn't remember doing it, but I must have covered my butt with my hands part of the time he was spanking me, thinking that would hurt less. But it really wasn't the splinters, or any other physical hurt that stayed with me.

Being accused of something awful when you're little—that's the worst part. Knowing you're innocent, yet unable to convince the people who matter the most. Your parents, the ones who normally protect you, become angry and uncaring—and that transformation has a strange, almost supernatural power. As a helpless kid, you feel like you're trapped by some horrible magic spell, or that your mind has opened up to some sinister force.

That's how it struck me, at least. I never forgot that feeling.

So it was rough to see Mattie in the same position. Hell, Lynn was even scaring *me* a little bit, and I knew this approach was all part of her strategy. A kid couldn't figure that out, though—wouldn't be world-wise enough to realize his mom was acting severe and angry for now, but as soon as this incident blew over things would be back to normal and she'd love him again, would laugh and smile and make his lunches and drive him to the after-school games. Instead, what Mattie understood in that moment, that rage flashing in his mother's eyes, told him: *You are not the sweet child I gave birth to. You are a liar, and you've committed horrible, unspeakable crimes. You are an evil, possessed thing. I have always hated you, even though I pretended otherwise. The next time I say I love you, I will be thinking about killing you. If I smile, it is because I imagine holding your head under water or pushing you in front of a car or sticking a knife into your throat and twisting it.*

You'll think my imagination's a little overactive here, I can guess, but maybe that's my point. When a little kid gets yelled at by his mom and dad, who knows what goes through his mind. Parents don't spank their kids anymore, and that's fine, but we hurt them in other ways. We can't help it.

So yeah, I knew Lynn said not to undermine her, but I needed to give poor Mattie something to hold on to. Some reassurance that things would be okay, no matter what.

I winked at him.

A private signal. Wait out the storm. Dad will help you fix it later.

An almost imperceptible calm washed over him. He didn't give me away, kept nodding at his mother's comments, but a little gleam appeared in his eyes. A sidelong glance that indicated he didn't feel trapped anymore. I was glad I rescued him.

"We're not getting anywhere," Lynn said. "You don't seem to realize how serious this is. Here's what I'm thinking, though. We'll talk to your sister, and maybe that will change my mind, but I don't expect it will. What I'm thinking is, we're going to have to cancel Halloween. No trick-or-treating, no costumes and decorations, no candy, no monster movies. Nothing."

She finally got him. Mattie had held up so well, like a little soldier, but now he pretty much fell apart, started crying and bawling. You can't. You can't. Oh, no. Please. Please, no.

Broke my heart.

Amber waited in our bedroom, and she would have heard her brother's wails even through the closed door. She must have thought we were torturing him.

Her turn next.

LYNN   X

WHEN CHILDREN are in crisis, and their parents can't form a united front to deal with it, wouldn't you agree that's another sign the marriage is in trouble?

I don't even need an answer, Mr. Therapist. Asking the question is enough.

My plan was for me to be the one who got tough with Matt, since Harris was always such a pushover with that boy.

I don't know how he expects his son will grow into a responsible adult without clear-cut rules to guide him.

Letting Harris try the "bad cop" role with Amber afterward was a kind of test.

I wanted to see if he could be firm but fair with her, maybe adapt some of the stern phrases I'd used so effectively with Matt.

Whatever happened, I'd learn something, right?

I'd figure out if Harris is the kind of person who could raise our kids.

Maybe earn some of *my* respect for a change. You need to respect the person you share your life with.

So we went to talk to Amber, who still sat on the corner of our bed.

Our bedroom was exactly as we'd left it, which didn't surprise me.

In contrast, Matt would have paced the room while he waited, opened and reopened the blinds, looked into our end tables, found something to read or borrowed some of Harris's spare change and tiddledywinked it across the bedspread.

Amber hadn't moved at all. Not even to get a Kleenex or two to wipe the tears away from her face.

She looked up, her eyes and nose red. She focused on me, and I just shook my head back and forth without saying a word.

Get this right, Harris. She's our best shot at the truth.

Matt can be sneaky, but Amber wants to be a good girl. Be smart. Smarter than a little kid.

I was actually rooting for him. I mean, I was expecting Harris to mess it up, but I hoped he'd surprise me.

Isn't that what happens in the last stages of a relationship?

You don't want to admit it's nearing the end.

You can't bear to think you've thrown so much of your life away.

That's why you don't tell the other person it's over.

You fool yourself. You keep waiting and hoping they'll do better, despite the mounting evidence to the contrary.

"What are we going to do with you, little lady?"

Harris moved closer to indicate he was in charge, which was good, but it was exactly the same question he'd ask when she spilled her drink or forgot to buckle her seatbelt in the car.

That kind of shake-your-head bemusement didn't set the appropriate tone for a serious talk.

Amber just said, "I don't know," and wiped a stray tear from her face.

Don't let her manipulate you, Harris.

"No time for crying," he told her, and I was proud of him for a moment. "Nobody listened when that bird cried out. Birds can feel pain, you know."

Amber started bawling, then, at the thought of that poor bird. She's always loved animals. Really sensitive.

Her crying got so loud and out of control, it pretty much threw Harris off his game. He stammered, then went to get some Kleenex from the dresser. He apologized to her.

Apologized!

Such a sign of weakness. Harris practically looked ready to start crying himself.

"Now stop, will you, honey?" He held a tissue to her nose while she blew into it. "We're not gonna hurt you. Just tell us what happened. Did you or Mattie do it? Did you do it together? Maybe you didn't mean for things to go this far. Sometimes you play a joke, without thinking it through. You didn't mean to do it, did you honey? C'mon, tell us."

What kind of response did he expect now that he'd removed any threat from the get-go?

We're not gonna hurt you.

(Yes, I'm mocking him in a singsong voice as I write this.)

And then feeding Amber an easy excuse, so all she has to say now is "I didn't mean it, Daddy" or "Mattie just thought it would be funny. I fixed the costume and he put it on the widdle para-tweet."

It would serve Harris right if I'd pulled faces behind his back while he questioned her. Rolled my eyes a few times or stuck out my tongue.

Why not?

His incompetence made a mockery of the whole situation.

It's almost perverse the way Harris forgets or ignores what I've told him about kids.

Everything a parent says or does can have some lasting effect.

Everything.

If you pull back on enforcing rules, if you don't apply meaningful consequences at every stage, then you're teaching your children that mischievous, even evil behavior is acceptable—not just in the home, but in the world at large.

That's a pretty dangerous message.

Amber looked straight at me, like she'd pretty much given up on her father having any sense at all.

"I didn't do anything," she said. "But I'll take my punishment. Whatever you think is right."

The punishment I had in mind was to grab her and shake her, like I'd wanted to do with Matt earlier.

Shake her until she stopped crying.

Shake the smug, innocent expression from the kid's face until the truth rattled out.

But that would have been wrong. The one I really wanted to grab and shake was their father.

"Halloween is canceled," I said.

"Yeah, um, that's right." Harris trying to be forceful. "No candy or costumes. You mom told the same thing to Mattie, and I support her decision one hundred and ten percent."

Then he said something I didn't expect.

He said, "Amber, I want you to change that story you're writing. It can't be a Halloween story now. It needs to be *nice*. Considering what happened here today, we need you to write about something nice."

Not quite a save but rescued from the failing grade. He'd chosen a punishment that fit the situation. Turned the tragedy into an authentic "teachable moment."

But all in all, he had let me down again, which explains why I had to change my tactics.

I visited a little home-security shop in a part of town I've never been to before and hope to never visit again.

If anyone needs all of the home security they can buy, it's the poor people who live around that shop.

I purchased the smallest hide-a-cam they had.

This sort of thing can be ordered from a hundred different websites.

I'm on the computer all day, so I know my way around.

I could easily find this kind of equipment online, then have it same-day delivered.

But anything you buy on the Internet leaves a trail.

I was afraid it would set off some red flag, put me on some kind of government watch list.

I'm not a terrorist or a criminal.

I'm just a concerned mom.

Besides, no need for Harris to see a credit card bill for Uncle Ed's Home Security Boutique and ask what that's all about.

If I never found anything, if our kids were the nice normal kids we'd all like to believe, there'd be no reason anybody would have to know about the camera.

I wouldn't ever have to tell Harris.

Wouldn't even have to write it down in my journal.

This camera is so small that I won't even know it's there when I'm in the room.

Sometimes you just have to be proactive to get things done, that's all.

So while the kids were at school, I hid the tiny battery-powered camera in their room.

The lens was pointed to the area between their beds, so it could monitor the majority of the room.

Setting everything up took some trial and error on my part since I had no instructions, but I've gotten pretty good at figuring out poorly conceived programs thanks to my job, and eventually I discovered the camera was putting out a decent WiFi signal.

I downloaded some software, and with a few clicks the computer was recording and storing the live feed from the camera.

After that, it was a matter of waiting and biding my time.

I didn't need to wait long, though.

That evening, the kids retired to their bedroom during family time.

Since the computer was in the living room and I didn't want Harris to know what I had done yet, I couldn't watch the live stream, but the manufacturer's website said twenty-four hours of footage would be stored on the computer.

I continued through the evening routine like normal and then, after Harris fell asleep, I snuck out to the living room to the computer.

I opened the software, which featured a giant magnifying glass on the logo screen, and began to fast-forward through the footage from the daytime when there was no one in the room.

I stopped fast-forwarding when family time rolled around, the door opened, and the kids entered the room.

I don't know what I had been expecting, but there wasn't anything alarming on the recording.

After ten minutes, I almost turned the computer off.

Both kids sat on the floor by their beds, their backs to the camera.

Matt was reading a book and Amber was cutting some of her craft paper from the "Your Creative Kids!" kit we bought her last year.

The kit was a little plastic suitcase that held all kinds of paper, tons of pens and markers and colored pencils, child-safe scissors, glue, tape, ribbons, various swatches of fabric, three types of glitter, rubber bands, and other materials for drawing, painting, and creating works of art.

Remembering my argument with Harris, I felt pretty silly about my concerns.

Actually, I felt worse than silly. What kind of mother spies on her children?

Just as I was about to close the software and delete it from the computer, Amber handed something to Matt, who extended his hand and took it without ever turning his head.

The knife certainly wasn't from the "Your Creative Kids!" kit.

The blade was way too sharp.

What disturbed me was the casual way Matt used it.

He was a small child holding a tool meant for a grown-up, so the proportions were awkward, but Matt's arm sawed back and forth, his elbow lifting high with each arc.

Next to him Amber mimed a similar motion in the air.

From the angle, Matt's body blocked what he was cutting.

All I could see was Amber's fascinated expression.

The more I squinted at the low-resolution screen, the more I noticed things they shouldn't have in their room. Halloween decorations, which I'm sure they haven't created themselves.

They look like the store-bought decorations from last year's party.

They knew I'd forbidden Halloween decorations, and they certainly knew better than to play with sharp, dangerous tools.

And for a moment it made me think: *These aren't my kids.*

My kids would never do such things.

HARRIS

"IT DOESN'T prove anything about the Durkinses' bird," my wife said. "But it proves I was right to be worried."

"What it proves is that you've crossed the line." Before my alarm had buzzed me awake, Lynn had shaken my shoulder and insisted I follow her into the den. She began pestering me to watch something on her computer, but the more she explained, the angrier I got. Matt and Amber were still asleep in their room, and I yelled almost loud enough to wake them. I couldn't believe how badly Lynn had violated our kids' privacy. "If they win, they win. You're not allowed to cheat."

"It's not cheating. We're their parents."

"Kids still have rights. You need to play fair."

Admittedly, I made up a lot of these rules, based on how I felt as a child during various battles with my own parents. From my way of thinking, a kid has to have a decent shot at winning—maybe learn to bear up under questioning, keep the story straight. If your son or daughter passes the harsh interrogation, you can't keep going back again and again until they break. You can't go all Truman and Hiroshima on them with your punishments, either. And you can't be all-seeing and all-knowing. It's just not fair.

What Lynn had done was hide a camera in the kids' bedroom. She'd recorded them and stored the files on the family computer where anyone could find them by accident.

She'd chosen some clips for me, but I refused to watch them. The program was open and displaying some still thumbnail images ready to be clicked on, but I wouldn't look at the screen.

"You need to know, Harris. You're turning a blind eye."

"Stop it." Now I was loud enough for the whole building to hear. "What you're doing is wrong. I'll have no part of it."

On one level, I understood my wife's frustration. She couldn't prove Matt's guilt, and in her mind that didn't mean he was innocent—it meant the boy was getting the better of her. Back when I was in middle school, my mom convinced herself my friends and I were smoking pot. She asked me again and again, she searched my jacket pockets when I got home from school; she practically tore my room apart one day, emptying dresser drawers and turning books upside down and shaking them over the carpet. All for nothing. Mom was so angry—when actually she should have been *happy* her suspicions weren't confirmed. Instead, she decided her teenage son was too clever and liked me a little less for that.

If my mom had spied on me, the outcome might have been different—but I don't think that tactic would have been good for either of us. As I continually tried to get my wife to understand, kids need their privacy. They need to feel trusted, even (especially?) when they didn't fully deserve that trust.

I thought about that private detective who'd been spying on Joanne Huff. If Joanne was cheating her insurance company, that was certainly wrong. But it's one thing to drive by her apartment once in a while, maybe sit at a bench across the street and peer over the top of a newspaper. It's another thing to move into the apartment building to plant mechanical eyes and ears for around-the-clock surveillance. He was *in* her apartment, for all intents and purposes. Invisible. Uninvited.

It was like he was haunting her.

However that detective died, whatever happened to his body afterward…I was beginning to think he deserved it.

"Promise me you'll get rid of them," I said. Meaning the camera and microphone, but for a moment Lynn blanched like I'd told her to get rid of the children.

"Not yet," she said. "I've almost got the answers I need. Another day or two."

How much time did she spend watching them? While she worked from home, she could keep a screen open on her computer—review the previous day's coloring session, eavesdrop on their after-dinner conversations. Watch them sleeping in their beds.

The idea sickened me, so I really lit into her, taking a moral high ground—which I didn't usually do. "That's the end," I yelled. "It's over."

"You don't get to decide."

The tension between us was pretty thick. I imagined Mattie and Amber cowering in their rooms, fingers plugged in their ears, and finally I lowered my voice. "Look, I'm not the strictest parent in the world. That's why you need to listen. If what you're doing bothers even *me,* doesn't that prove it's bad?"

"You're no help in raising these kids," she said. "I can never depend on you. Don't think I didn't see you yesterday, Harris. Don't think I didn't see you wink at him."

"What? No. When?" I held up my hands like I didn't understand, then pointed to the side of my face. "I get a twitch sometimes."

Lynn took a deep breath. I half worried maybe she was going to hit me. She had that counting-to-ten expression, but at the four-count she spoke in a calmer voice, making what she considered was a reasonable request. "I want the key to Matt's locked drawer."

"Oh, come on. Even if I had it—"

"Nobody's stupid enough to give a kid a lock without keeping a copy of the key. Not even you. Give it to me."

"You're crazy." Not the smartest thing to say, especially when your wife's already on the edge of losing it. Her eyes went wide, mouth open with no sound coming out, but maybe some steam coming out her ears. "Crazy," I repeated.

Then I stormed out of the apartment, slamming the door behind me.

I HADN'T taken time to get my jacket and the late evening was pretty chilly. I moved briskly to keep warm, following one of my typical routes through the property.

Times like this, I cleared my head just by walking. I wouldn't think about work, my neighbors, my wife and kids. If I passed an outdoor lamp with a dead bulb, I didn't make a mental note to replace it tomorrow; I didn't count cars in the parking lots or wonder why the shades were drawn in unit 7C. All that mattered was the ground beneath, each shift from sidewalk to road, from grass to dirt path. My feet followed a memorized route, guided by vague cues in my peripheral vision. If I wanted, I could navigate parts of the property with my eyes closed. I'd even tried that a couple of times for short stretches.

I want to address a notion most people have about handymen. Mainly, that we're arrogant. We know how to fix things and think of all the residents as idiots who put metal forks in their microwaves, Kotex in their toilets, and comb their longest hairs into the shower drains. They break equipment regularly, as if they take perverse joy in ruining their living space.

I've got a bit of that prejudice against tenants, I'll confess. But there's another repairman's trait I'd never quite fallen into: I call it "the handyman fallacy." It's the mistaken sense that because you repair appliances or nail a few boards back in place, the buildings and various fixtures actually belong to you. You're the artist, maybe, and the repairs are your signature. In this mindset, when people break stuff, it's like a personal affront: How *dare* you scratch this section of wallpaper, *my* wallpaper; how *dare* you overload my washing machines with your stinking clothes.

I mean, sure, I'd judge people for being stupid. But if they wanted to break parts of their home, so they had to wait days or weeks for me to saunter by and fix it, that was their problem. Nothing for me to get upset about.

Never had that arrogant sense of being everyone's boss, of owning the place. What would be the point? We were all living in apartments. None of us owned anything, really.

My pathways were the exception, though. Walking them, memorizing them, those routes became mine. That night's particular path: Eleven steps on the sidewalk, then a detour between buildings 8 and 9, emerging with the park bench at the corner of my eye and our largest elm blocking the moonlight, and I crunched through fallen leaves until I hit the foot-worn path that led to a chain-link fence, one section bent back to create a shortcut to University Road. I turned, following the stretch of the fence, an easy path through everyone's backyard, and if people glanced out their kitchen windows they might say "That's Harris on his rounds," or wonder how I could see without a flashlight, how I crossed uneven footing almost like I was dancing, or walking from stone to stone above the froth of a rushing river.

As usual, the late-night walk calmed me. I wasn't fighting with Lynn anymore, wasn't worrying about our kids. Only the path.

I closed my eyes for a moment.

And I was lost.

I froze, overcome with the horrible sense that my next step would be off a steep cliff. My foot would trigger a landmine, a bear trap would snap metal teeth into my ankle. A loose covering of grass would collapse and I'd fall into a pit lined with sharp wooden spikes.

In the still night air a voice seemed to whisper like the rustle of leaves. *Don't leave them. Don't leave them with her.*

Standing motionless, I was struck anew by the October chill. Why had that thought come to me? I'd fought with Lynn, didn't like her idea of spying on the kids. The notion was unexpected and foreign to me, like a hazard placed along a familiar path. But otherwise she was a great mother. She'd never harm our children.

I knew my wife wouldn't hurt me, either. Wouldn't really have thrown a punch or cat-scratched me in the midst of our disagreement.

I knew that.

But as I fast-walked back to our apartment, eyes open and afraid I'd trip the whole time, I thought I heard the laugh of a witch, followed by the screams of children as they were stuffed into an oven.

💀

LYNN SAT at her desk, calm as could be. She didn't acknowledge me as I entered the apartment, but I noticed that she quickly shifted the task windows on her computers.

I went to the kids' room. The door was closed when I got there, and I knocked on it before testing the knob. Locked.

"You guys okay?"

"Why wouldn't we be," Amber said from the other side of the door. It felt good to hear her voice, even though she has this maddening way of phrasing questions as statements—and often barely listened if I attempted to answer. In this case, I didn't have a reasonable reply. *Oh, I've just got this bad feeling. About your mother. Prove me wrong, would you? Please?*

"Mattie in there with you?"

"It's his room, too, isn't it."

"Hey, Mattie." I rattled the door handle. Matt didn't respond. Instead, I heard a couple of drawers open and shut, papers shuffled, quick footsteps on the carpet.

Funny thing: It sounded like the frantic movements their mother would make whenever she cleaned the room. I'd just seen Lynn in the den, so that was impossible.

Except, in a sense, she *was* in the room. Her eyes and ears.

"Let me in."

Amber scurried away from the door and another set of footsteps approached. Heavy steps. An adult's tread.

A click, but the door didn't open. The footsteps retreated.

I reached for the knob and this time it turned. I pushed the door open and entered the kids' room.

Amber sat at the edge of her bed, a schoolbook open on her lap. I got the sense that she hadn't actually been reading it.

Mattie was at his desk, sketchbook turned to a fresh page and his box of markers ready.

The room had its usual division: Matt's bed made and every item in its proper place; Amber's covers pulled back and stuffed animals and toys and papers scattered on the bed and along the floor. The same way the room always looked, but maybe a little "off." Almost like they'd staged it for my benefit.

"Your mother wonders what you guys do in here."

"Oh, homework and reading and drawing. What else could we do." Again, Amber phrased her question like a flat statement.

"We can't watch a scary movie. Mom won't let us." Matt didn't turn to face me. Apparently the blank page was more interesting to him.

"There's other kinds of movies." I crossed to their fifteen-inch television with built-in DVD player. I'd borrowed some of the Stillbrook supply wood to build a TV stand, with slots below to hold their various DVDs. "Lots of cartoons here. Superhero stuff. Comedies." As I pretended to scan their library of movies, I was actually trying to figure out where Lynn might have hidden the spy camera. This seemed a likely placement, alongside other electronic equipment.

"We've seen all of those," Matt said.

"A hundred times."

"A hundred? You're way ahead of me, Amber. I don't think I've seen *any* movie a hundred times." I followed the cords behind the TV stand, checked where they met the power strip and the wall socket. Nothing out of the ordinary.

Now I wished I'd allowed Lynn to show me one of the recordings, since I could have judged from the angle where the camera was hidden. Matt's items were so meticulously placed, he likely would have noticed any new knickknack added to his bookshelves. On Amber's side, I picked up the nearest stuffed creature—a brown bear. "Does this thing talk?" I peered into its black plastic eyes to check for a small camera lens. I shook it, then turned it upside down. "In my day, a teddy bear might have a string coming out of his butt. You pulled the string, and the bear would talk."

"What would he say?"

Mattie chimed in with an answer. "'Get that string out of my butt.'"

The kids laughed, and I joined them. "You're right, Mattie. That would have been pretty uncomfortable."

I checked a few more plush toys, dropping them in place after I found nothing. In Amber's dollhouse, the doll figure for the dad was missing a leg and was all scratched up—from where Mattie must have accidentally stepped on it. There was a kids' room in the dollhouse, too. The house front was shorn off, so anybody could look inside. So exposed and vulnerable. A giant hand could grab the dolls at any moment; a giant foot could grind them into the ground.

"How long is Mom going to stay mad at us?" Mattie asked.

"We're both mad," I told him. "Remember?"

"Probably until Halloween," Mattie said. "Definitely that long."

I decided to correct my earlier statement. "We're not mad. Just punishing you for what you did." They were both quiet at that, not protesting their innocence as they had the day before. I reminded myself that they'd heard me fighting with their mother. Similar family fights had a profound effect on me when I was their age. I worried that my parents hated each other, had decided to get a divorce, or to do away with the source of all their problems: me. Scary stuff for little kids to overhear, and I wished I could apologize to Mattie and Amber.

I crossed to the window, then pulled aside the dinosaur curtains and put my palm flat against the cool glass. Because of the internal light, it was impossible to see outside. There could easily have been someone looking in. How about a giant face pressed close to the other side of the window. Or a ghost, able to float outside the second-floor room, waiting until bedtime to shimmer through glass and wood and brick, hovering over the sleeping kids to steal their dreams. Or a creature with claws and batlike wings that flap loudly as it hovers in place. It's there now, calling to me, asking me to open the window. Open it.

I placed my hand on the metal latch. It was fastened shut.

"Tell me more about Halloween, Dad." I hadn't heard him move, but Mattie was standing beside me. I noticed his reflection in the window.

"No. If your mother found out, I'd get in trouble."

Lynn could have been watching me right then, on her remote monitor. Since I was being recorded, I had to be on my best behavior. Be a good parent. Her idea of one, at least.

I imagined Lynn as a floating ghost. I imagined her with wings, or wearing a black cape with a red lining. Her eyes grew large; her breath steamed over sharp teeth to fog the children's bedroom window.

LYNN X

THIS ISN'T supposed to be a dream journal. Those are kind of silly anyway.

I never tell people my dreams. They're so random and meaningless. Writing them down implies they're worthy of other people's time.

And your time is expensive, Mr. Therapist.

But then again, this dream definitely relates to other things we've been talking about. My marriage. And the more recent topic: concern about my children.

I like to think of myself as a good medical patient, so that means I need to anticipate questions you might ask. I need to select things you can interpret.

In some ways, I'm having to do your job for you, almost like I'm an amateur psychologist myself.

Everybody knows that psychologists love to interpret dreams.

Maybe this dream gives you access to my subconscious. That's something you want, right?

What I ate before bedtime:

Dinner: Spaghetti with meat sauce on the side, plus a vegetable and cream sauce for Amber since she's too sensitive to eat animal products. I had some of each.

A bag salad on the side, with added green peppers, garlic croutons, and fake bacon bits.

I fixed all of this myself, for the record, even though it was Harris's night.

Tick that in one of the irritation columns: Sometimes he has a busy day, which supposedly sometimes wears him out and means he's unable to do his housework that evening.

I have my share of busy days, too, but since I work from home that doesn't count. Easier for me to get dinner started, since "I'm home anyway."

Dessert: Rice pudding made with extra rice from last night's stir-fry. Mixed with milk, sugar, cinnamon, and raisins.

Just before bed, I snuck down to the kitchen and had a few extra spoonfuls of rice pudding.

Wasn't much left, so not worth saving, and I put the container right into the dishwasher.

So nothing spicy and a modest late snack that likely settled my stomach rather than upsetting it.

Judging by diet, no reason at all why I should have a nightmare.

Judging by my life, though? It's a wonder I can even get to sleep at all.

Our kids did a terrible thing, but Harris makes it worse.

Not just because he can't see Matt's guilt, so clear from the way he reacted to our questions.

Amber's innocence so clear, too, and yet she's covering up for her brother.

That's almost as bad, isn't it? I'm afraid she's turning against her own gentle nature.

Her love of animals, at least.

But Harris is the worse problem because he's practically given our children permission to tell lies.

With the camera I've placed, we have a simple way to uncover the truth. Harris refuses to look. It's as if the truth doesn't matter to him.

He made such a big deal yesterday about how awful it was to hide the camera in their room.

He *lawyered* me, almost: talked about our kids' privacy. How wrong it was for me to spy on them.

Not spying. They're our kids. We have to watch what they do.

It's part of our job as parents.

But Harris really raised his voice, treated me like I was some kind of evil villain.

The witch in *Snow White* looking through her magic mirror.

He wasn't right. I knew he wasn't right. But it still hurt to be spoken to that way.

All because of a camera. A tiny electronic device that Amber and Matt never need to know about.

So no, my dinner didn't upset my stomach and give me a bad dream. Harris did.

Instead of reading my book for a while, I simply turned off my bedside light. That's how upset I was.

I turned my back to Harris and closed my eyes tight.

Off and on throughout the evening, I had checked the video feed of the kids' room to see what they were doing, which is probably where a lot of the dream images came from.

They huddled close and their backs were usually to the camera, but they spent most of their time drawing or cutting paper designs I couldn't quite distinguish.

The black-and-white image was fairly low resolution, so it was hard to see.

At one point they took a break and Amber did a little rag-doll dance that was cute.

While she danced, Matt walked around her, pointing at the floor with his finger as if it was a magic wand that could outline a circle in the carpet.

It was a cute little scene, and I saved that section of the file to watch again later.

I'd spent so much time watching those little black-and-white screens, I could practically still see them when I closed my eyes to sleep.

I mostly dream in black-and-white, also, so that might explain why things blurred together for me.

In my dream, I watch my computer screen.

On my headset, a customer's voice breaks through.

"Everything was working fine this morning. I can't understand how it's changed. Can you explain that to me?"

Patient as I can be, the same way I always am with customers, I say, "I might not be able to tell you what you did wrong, but I can help you fix it. Does that sound good?"

From there I had the "service script" of things to try, starting with rebooting their system—a cold boot, then a warm boot—then I'd walk them through a check of their RAM and graphics card and how to temporarily disable their virus software to apply the latest patch.

The script works like a flow chart on my screen, and I check-box each step when completed.

Sometimes I get bored saying the same phrases over and over, so I might vary the order, or maybe add a joke or other pleasantry.

Basically make the experience more fun for me and for the customer.

In my dream I barely look at the service script and recite the steps from memory.

I press Alt + Tab, and the script goes away, replaced by the grainy view of our children's bedroom.

I'm aware that it's nighttime, since that is when we dream, but it doesn't strike me as odd that I'd be handling an after-hours service call.

It does strike me as odd that Matt and Amber are awake. They have school tomorrow.

Their bedroom light is on, so I don't need to switch to the night-vision mode.

"What are you doing?" I speak to their figures on the screen, knowing they can't hear me.

"I'm doing just what you told me," the customer replies on my headset.

"You shouldn't be messing with that."

Amber is swinging something like a sword or a saw or board. It's so heavy she can barely lift it, but she swings it nonetheless.

She swings it at Matt's head.

"I only clicked on the 'Uninstall' icon," the customer says. "Should I click 'Cancel'?"

"You don't know," I shout at the screen. "You're messing with things you couldn't possibly understand."

On the grainy screen, the sword or saw or board hits Matt on the head and he crumples to the ground.

Amber drops her weapon, and in some strange distortion of the camera image, her feet seem to rise from the floor as if she's levitating.

From my headset I hear, "*You* should know. *You're* the one who's supposed to understand."

"Not you," I say. "Not you."

Meaning *I'm not talking to you, idiot customer.*

My job doesn't matter anymore, because my children are in their room and one of them has tried to kill the other.

They're not themselves. Amber isn't herself. Not you, Amber. Not you.

And I wake up in my bed and it's dark.

Black-and-white like I'm still dreaming, grainy like I'm still watching a security feed on my computer.

That is what's happening.

It's *our* bedroom on a computer screen, but I'm watching from the precise angle where I've hidden the camera in the kids' room.

I'm peering down at myself from the top of our doorframe.

I look confused. Harris sleeps next to me, covers to his neck, oblivious.

There's a dotted line down the center of our bed. Harris's side of the room is perfectly clean, but the sheets and blanket on my side are bunched up at my feet.

My books and clothes and toiletries are tossed about my half of the room, as if a tornado has struck.

On Harris's side, the curtains are pulled tight over the window.

On my side, the curtain rod has fallen and the shade has flipped up.

There's movement outside the window.

Something like the moon but with a shade over it opening and closing.

Blinking. A giant eye, looking in.

It feels like we're in Amber's dollhouse.

It's Amber's giant eye looking in, but then she's pushed away so Matt can take his turn.

I feel how awful it is to be spied upon.

And as if that's the lesson of the dream, the image flickers and I'm looking out of my own eyes again, in bed.

But I'm not awake.

Because Amber and Mattie walk into our room.

They have to lean down to fit through the door, and they walk to the foot of our bed.

They tilt their heads so they won't brush against the ceiling.

They are big and powerful, the way parents should be. They are so large they could crush us in our beds.

Harris finally wakes. He pulls the covers down and sits up in bed. He says to Giant Matt: "I'm still your favorite, aren't I?"

Amber looms over my side of the bed, and I feel helpless. Her voice is loud but still childlike. "If you had to choose," she asks, "which one of us would you want to kill?"

That's all I remember from the dream.

Pretty strange, huh? I guess you can do your therapist magic on it, come up with all kinds of interpretations.

Maybe it lets you know how my subconscious mind works.

Like I said, I thought it would be the kind of thing you'd want to know.

But I really don't see why you'd need access to my subconscious. I've been completely honest with you. I'm not hiding anything.

In computer language, I'm WYSIWYG. What you see is what you get.

And part of that means I have to follow through on my threats.

When I said No Halloween, I meant No Halloween.

Yet I was in a bit of a pickle.

I saw things on the hidden camera and knew they had those decorations in there, but I hadn't "officially" caught them at it.

If I went into their room and went straight to their hiding place, they'd know something was up.

They might figure out I'd been watching them.

I'm not letting Harris make me feel bad about the camera. Parents should use every tool at their disposal. I don't feel ashamed about it.

But I don't want to play my hand just yet.

The camera provides useful information for me...as long as the kids don't know it's there.

There's a microphone that picks up sound, too.

Most of the time, kids ramble on about nothing.

They're good at multitasking, if you think about it. They can color or cut or glue things together while they talk about something completely unrelated.

The soundtrack to their video feed usually seemed out of sync.

They didn't speak about what they were drawing or cutting or putting together.

At times Amber would hum a wordless melody but never any song I could recognize.

Once, Matt joined in. He'd been around his sister so much, I guess "Amber's Greatest Hits" got stuck in his head.

Matt's accompaniment sounded more like lyrics, but the recording wasn't strong enough for me to distinguish any words.

Maybe they made up their own language, just to sing in. Wouldn't that be funny?

Anyway, I found the audio feed mostly useless.

Plus, if I listened during the day, it would interfere with my work headset.

After the first thirty seconds of a call, I could ninety-nine percent predict what customers would say, but I still had to listen to them while I was on the clock.

That said, in one of my random checks of the audio from the hidden camera, I got lucky and overheard Matt make a comment about me and about school tomorrow.

I had forgotten that the classes always do something to acknowledge Halloween.

The teacher reads a scary story and gives out candy. Some of the teachers even wear a costume and they encourage kids to do the same.

Last year Ms. Linder dressed as Dumbledore from Harry Potter and the kids all laughed at a thirty-five-year-old woman with a long gray beard hanging from her chin.

"Mother forgot about that," Matt said to Amber. "We'll still get to celebrate Halloween at school."

Bingo.

A fairly memorable detail from last year, and they'd never guess I needed a hidden microphone to recall it.

As I tucked my children in at bedtime, I announced that they were staying home from school tomorrow.

"No Halloween," I said. "Here *or* there."

Actions have consequences, after all.

That would teach Matt for thinking he'd outsmarted me.

Plus, it would give me a whole day at home to watch over them.

I'm starting to think I can't trust them out of my sight anymore.

From: Jessica Shepard
To: Jacob Grant

DON'T TOY with the Halloween Children, Jacob. They know you tried to call me. Don't come here, please, just don't. I told you it's too late for me. **The Halloween Children are EVERYWHERE.**
Don't contact me again. PLEASE LEAVE ME ALONE.

—Jess

P.S. Plans have changed, and I hope you have a costume ready. If not, I have something you can borrow. Click below for a special ecard invitation. Remember, you should NEVER click on an attachment unless it's from someone you know and trust. You're safe with me, of course! ;)

<<attachment: invitation10_31.exe>>

HARRIS   X

HALLOWEEN MORNING, my task list from Shawna was ridiculous. Two pages of ridiculous. If I'd actually planned to finish everything, I wouldn't have a spare minute to myself.

I decided to complete what I could at my own pace. More important, I promised myself I'd stop in at the apartment periodically to check on our kids. Lynn had been acting so strange lately, obsessed with Halloween, denying the holiday as her idea of punishment, consequence, whatever she called it. In my experience, if you put a lid on something, you actually create a pressure cooker—which explained all the blowups I had with my parents growing up and also explained why I tried to be so easygoing with Mattie and Amber. Kids need their parents to be calm, and Lynn was having trouble meeting that need.

I hoped to provide a normal parent's kind of surveillance. You know, not the twenty-four-hour, Big Brother hidden-camera type Lynn was currently experimenting with, but the healthy way parents have always watched over their kids: making sure they don't hurt themselves, that they're kind to each other, maybe that they learn a thing or two about history or about other people or how the world works. Or just hang around with them and goof off once in a while—exercise a sense of humor, instead of being so serious all the time. That was the main thing I hoped to pass along to my children.

That was my plan, at least. Somehow the time got away from me.

Every task was frustrating. The way Shawna filled the list, I suspected she'd been saving the worst to dump on me the last day of the month, almost like she was trying to get me to quit. Dreaded shelf replacements in not one but three units—each board a non-standard size that needed to be measured, cut, placed, adjusted, then placed again. Some clogged sinks just on the edge of needing professional plumbing, and in the first job I broke a rusted pipe and had to keep the family's water turned off. The other sink had the most disgusting hair clog I'd ever seen: I snaked the drain and pulled back a slick wet thing like the arm of a drowned dog. In that case, the newly cleared drain unclogged with a spray of black gunk, and I had to repaint part of the wall above the sink. As the eggshell paint began to dry, the black gunk started to fade through, and I had to promise another layer the next day before the resident would let me leave.

Honestly, I felt like I was building things merely to take them back apart. Lots of fruitless labor, with no improved results.

Then there were the pest traps. For some reason, Shawna decided it was time to inventory them. All of them. I'd labeled the traps on the bottom—for good reason, since it kept tenants from spotting the dates and querying if they'd expired. But that meant I'd have to lift each trap from the dark corner where I'd set it to check underneath. Well, there was something *on* most of the traps—and not the critters we were trying to catch. Some kind of glue or syrup drizzled out of the opening or overtop the plastic casing, and it got on my hands or, when I moved the trap with a screwdriver or pliers or a wooden dowel, it stuck to *that,* too, and then to my foot as I tried to separate the pieces. A real nuisance, and after a few encounters I sniffed my fingertips and the chemical odor made me worry it was some leaked poison, applied by an exasperated tenant hoping to make these cosmetic traps into something more effective. Had I rubbed the poison beneath an itching eye, or pressed some of it into my hair or dragged it along my lower lip?

In the midst of this paranoid freak-out, in a dark spider-webby nook beneath the basement stairwell of building ten, my work cell rang. On instinct I reached for it, my fingers sticking to the lining of my pocket as I dug into it and closed around the buzzing, vibrating phone. I swiped my finger over the unlock screen. The glass felt like sandpaper, and I imagined a layer of my skin shredding off with the aggressive swipe.

If I'd seen the caller ID in time, I wouldn't have answered it.

Joanne Huff's voice rose shrill from the speaker. "Harris, there's a smell in the building. Like a mouse crawled between the walls and died. I can't tell you where it's coming from, but it's there. Do you hear me?"

"Yeah." Initially I'd held the phone away from my ear to keep it from sticking to my face, but I brought it closer to speak. My lips brushed against the mouthpiece. Closer to my nostrils, the chemical smell grew stronger. "Busy."

"Come and see for yourself. Smell for yourself, I mean. Right away."

"Can't. At the other end of the property." A new odor seemed to waft from the phone, an awful concoction of poison and rot.

Her illness. Joanne's mystery illness, transmitted through the phone. It occurred to me then that Joanne was smelling her own decay.

"Right away, Harris. It's not bad yet, but I know it will get worse."

"Seems like that's always the way, doesn't it?"

"What? What did you say?"

I hung up. Joanne would call the office next, which was fine with me. Let Shawna deal with her for a change.

LIKE I said, I planned to stop home periodically and check on Lynn and the kids, but I felt like my work tasks sabotaged me. The way Shawna prioritized the items took me to the opposite edge of the community, too out-of-the-way for me to visit my family.

I thought about them, though. I wondered what my kids were doing. Perhaps they fantasized about Halloween and all the candy and the fun scares they could be enjoying. Or perhaps they treated the day like a punishment, as Lynn expected from them.

At the very least, I hope they enjoyed the time home from school—treated it like a snow day, a gift of freedom, the hours suddenly and gloriously all their own.

I'd like to think that. A snow day is much better than a sick day. Bored and napping and waiting for a dose of cough syrup or clear broth—the hours falling into dismal patterns.

At one point I was certain I'd heard Mattie's laugh. I was getting fresh bulbs from the storage closet in building four and the laugh seemed to carry in the wind, as might happen in fall and winter when the leaves didn't dampen sound; and midday, with few cars roaring past, the televisions and stereos mostly silent. Probably it wasn't Mattie, but it sounded so much like him.

Later, when I crossed the parking lot to building eight, I saw Amber out of the corner of my eye. She ran behind the building toward the gap in the fence that led off our property. My eyes played tricks on me, though. It must have been another of the neighborhood girls, in a blue dress similar to one of Amber's—though, come to think of it now, any girl Amber's age should have been in school at the time.

But the kids were home being punished. Their mother never would have allowed either of them outside to play.

My phone buzzed again, and I pressed through my pocket to mute it. Cold wind whistled through barren branches. The phone continued to vibrate in my pocket.

Joanne's voice came through anyway.

"The smell is worse now. It's so bad I can almost notice it on my own clothing. It's everywhere, Harris."

I pressed the heel of my hand against my pocket, trying to muffle the phone, strangle it into silence.

LYNN   X

HALLOWEEN, FINALLY. Or *not* Halloween, as I've decreed it.

The kids seemed content to play in their room all day.

I tried to encourage them to watch TV in the den, for at least a little while, but they wouldn't budge.

Amber told me: "I don't want to bother you while you're working."

She sat at the edge of her unmade bed, surrounded by plush animals of all sizes. She talked mostly to a large stuffed bear rather than to me.

"You won't," I told her. "As long as you stay quiet."

"I'm not sure I can do that." Amber lifted the bear's front paws, making him dance in the air.

I laughed with her. "It's not healthy to stay cooped up in this room all day."

"We're fine," Matt said. "We're being punished."

"Suit yourself."

I stepped away, certain they'd get bored eventually and beg for a short reprieve from their prison.

As I headed back to my desk, I heard Matt's quick footsteps as he rushed to shut and lock their bedroom door.

I had a reason for wanting them to leave the room.

I wanted to do a quick search.

From watching the camera feeds, I had a pretty good idea where Matt hid the key to his locked drawer.

I was determined to get inside that drawer, even if it killed me.

That's just a figure of speech, as I'm sure you know. Not worth making a big Freudian deal over.

It was getting on ten-fifteen, which may not seem that long, but considering Amber wakes up at six-thirty, it's quite a stretch.

Factor in "kid time" where unoccupied minutes tick by extra slowly and I figured they were getting really stir-crazy.

On the video feed, they barely moved at all. They remained motionless for so long that I almost thought the recording had frozen, but the time in the corner of the screen kept moving. If I hit the side of the monitor, I wondered if that would make them move.

I get a fifteen-minute break midway through my morning shift, and another fifteen minutes in the afternoon.

I took off my headset for the morning break and headed to the kids' room.

"Open up." I beat an authoritarian knock on their closed door. "Fire drill."

Amber opened the door instantly. She must have been standing on the other side of it, waiting for my knock.

"We didn't hear a siren," she said.

Matt sat at his desk, back to me, in the same position he maintained on the recent video feed.

"No siren," I explained. "This is your mom's version of a fire drill. It's more of a 'nice day' drill. What that means is that you, both of you, need to play outside for a while. Until I call you back in."

Matt turned around in his chair. "I'm drawing," he said. "I'd rather stay here."

"Take your pad and markers outside if you want. You kids need some fresh air. That's an order."

"Yay, an order!" Amber was already past me and headed for the hallway.

"Don't forget your jacket," I called after her. "Bundle up."

Matt followed, dragging his feet to reinforce how unfair it was that I'd interrupted his punishment.

Once they were out the front door and on their way to the stairs, I returned to their bedroom, where I discovered that Matt had left his current sketchbook behind after all.

I flipped through the pages.

They were typical boy drawings: dinosaurs and airplanes and fire trucks, a few superheroes.

He was at the usual skill level for his age group, which is a nice way of saying they weren't very good. Okay to put under a refrigerator magnet but a long way from hanging in a museum.

The colors were effective, though.

He used all kinds of markers and pencils and did a decent job with shading.

Flowers appeared in a few places and unexpected bright colors.

I thought it was nice that Matt allowed his sister to add her contributions to some of his drawings.

That showed a new maturity on his part.

I returned the sketchpad, careful to align the binding with the left edge of the desk, exactly how I found it.

Next I took Matt's paint set from the hutch over his desk.

I unlatched the set and lifted the top layer.

I found a small silver key at the bottom of the brush compartment.

The hairs at the back of my neck seemed to stand up at that moment, the way they do when it feels like someone's watching.

I realized I was in direct view of the camera I'd hidden in their room.

And, yes, I felt a little guilty then.

As a parent, I was perfectly within my rights to search through my son's things, but I would have felt terrible if I'd been caught in the act.

This seemed more serious than watching through a camera lens from a safe distance.

Harris talked about "crossing the line."

I didn't agree with him about the camera, but maybe this was my idea of the line.

Maybe I was going too far. I could have just walked away. Left Matt his privacy.

But the key shone bright in my hand and it slid easily into the locked drawer.

Because it was *only* a drawer.

What could be so terrible in such a small space?

Matt was simply a child. He was small, too, with a small range of experiences.

What could be so terrible?

I pulled open the drawer.

I found more drawings in there, crafted with different skill. And depravity.

I was looking into my son's mind and I was horrified at what I saw.

Play outside for a while. Until I call you back in.

I didn't want to call my children back inside.

I was afraid of what I might have to do.

HARRIS   X

L ATE AFTERNOON, I needed supplies from our main storage area in six—
the building connected to my own. I definitely planned to visit Mattie
and Amber after I'd retrieved the boards and brackets I needed.

When I stepped down to the basement, the supply room was locked.
Not the individual storage units but the door to the entire room. Shawna
had done this, I guessed—and forgot to give me the key. I remember
thinking Shawna might be playing a sick joke. She overloaded me with
tasks, all leading up to my discovery that the locks have been changed.
That's how you tell somebody he's been fired, right? Lock him out of his
own workspace.

I rattled the knob. I considered breaking down the door, but if I wasn't
fired, I'd just end up having to fix it again. The way my day had been
going, creating additional useless work was the last thing I needed.

I considered what to do next. This was Joanne Huff's building. If I
wanted, I could have gone upstairs and checked for the smell that bothered her.

Nothing odorous down here except for the usual basement mildew and
the sickly sweet detergent and softeners from the nearby laundry room.

I held still, my hand on the locked door that wouldn't budge. The
building remained quiet, lacking the explosive squawks from behind

the Durkinses' door. They still didn't know what happened to their pet.

They also didn't know how I used to stand outside their door and whisper obscenities through the wood, hoping to teach the bird colorful phrases that would interrupt the family's evening calm. A harmless trick, if it ever worked.

Those phrases might have found an appropriate context as the animal screamed its worst, gagged and burning to death in our oven.

I felt a strange onrush of guilt then. About the bird but also about the other tenants and how I often spoke about them. My dislike of Shawna and her rules; the recent tension with Lynn. And our kids. I thought about our kids and I suddenly felt like I'd been whispering at *them* through a door, teaching them the wrong things to say, the worst ways to act.

Isn't that funny, for me to think that way, at that particular moment?

Maybe I got a little light-headed after working so hard the whole day. That poison I imagined had dripped off our mouse and roach traps, the smell of death Joanne Huff detected in the building. Paint fumes can also have that kind of effect. And maybe an odorless gas, too, like carbon monoxide or radon, a barely detectable hiss through some loose valve.

When people get carbon-monoxide poisoning, they don't even notice it. They just feel tired, drift off to sleep, and never wake.

If I slept, in that moment, what would I have dreamt?

My dreams would be of construction work. Hammering nails into wood. Tying ropes, painting backdrops. Cutting bizarre shapes with a hacksaw. Reaching into tight, sticky spaces, grabbing a hank of hair, and pulling with all my might.

THE BASEMENT was already dark, so I hadn't realized there'd been a power outage. The whole building was dark.

It was after six o'clock when I stepped outside. Twilight drifted toward a dark, moonless night.

Amber sometimes got scared in the dark. I hurried to our building next door, raced blindly up the stairs to our apartment.

The apartment was nearly pitch-black. I called out for them.

No answer.

Lynn and the kids were gone.

IF YOU'VE ever woken in the middle of the night in a sudden panic—grabbing for a lamp switch, the warm comfort of your wife's shoulder, a knife hidden under the mattress for protection—and before you move, you're overcome with fear that your fingers will close instead around the wet jaws of a wild animal, the tail of a rat, the limber bristled legs of a large spider...or maybe worst of all, you'd grab at nothing, because you're not in your room anymore, like that college prank where your hallmates carry your bed outside with you passed out on it, drop the bed in the middle of a baseball field, and abandon you.

If that late-night panic has ever happened to you, then you understand how I felt entering my home. That small familiar apartment now seemed alien. I bumped into a table that shouldn't have been inside the door, heard a wobble, then the drop and crash of a glass vase. I shouted for Lynn and Mattie and Amber but no answer. Since I'd left my toolkit outside the storage room, I didn't have my flashlight with me. I patted at the living room wall, found the light switch in what seemed a slightly different place, and flipped it to no effect.

The electricity was out. Of course I knew that, but it's still an odd sensation when these switches don't work as you expect. I tried it a few times anyway, maybe even mouthed "Huh?" to the apartment.

Perhaps I spoke aloud to fill the void. We always left a box fan running in the bedroom for background noise; our refrigerator made a constant low rattle, like the idling of an old car. The absence of these typical sounds unnerved me almost as much as the dark.

And obviously, a house with kids should never be completely silent. Amber's chatter and singsong, the scratch of Mattie's pencil on his sketchpad, the quick footsteps that stop just before I warn them not to run in the house. Faucets on and off, cereal poured into a bowl, soda into a glass. And Lynn, too, clicking at her computer keyboard, turning magazine pages, clearing her throat before she asks me a question.

Where could they have gone? If they left me a note, it was too dark to read it.

My wife should at least have phoned me.

Then I thought, *Maybe she did,* at the same time I also realized the screen of my phone could provide some reasonable light.

The phone seemed stuck in my pocket. When I pulled it out, only a faint glow rose from the front, white text on a black background, spelling out Joanne Huff on the ID screen. Random lines hatched through the faint letters, and as I slid my finger across in an attempt to wake the screen, I felt tiny ridges of cracked glass.

When Joanne called me the second time, I pressed down on my pocket to muffle her voice and I must have pressed too hard, breaking the phone.

The cracked white letters on the ID screen didn't help much, but I angled the phone ahead of me and squinted. In our kitchen we maintained an "emergency drawer" with candles and matches, so I headed that way.

My memory of the kitchen layout helped me avoid our table and chairs at the center, and I felt for the counter on the left side of the sink. Lynn's latest "As Seen on TV" contraption sat on the counter. She had a habit of ordering gimmick appliances, then using them only once—tortilla makers, mini-donut fryers, hash brown choppers. I couldn't remember the latest unnecessary purchase, but the hint of light outlined an appliance with a large glass dome at the top. I touched the glass and it was still warm. A hiss of steam shot up through some crack or nozzle, spraying a hot breath along the underside of my wrist. It smelled like cabbage and brussels sprouts.

I felt beneath the counter for the drawer handle and pulled. The drawer was stuck on its roller-track, so I had to jiggle and force it open. The contents rattled—not wax candles but metal clicking against metal. When I reached in, I cut my finger on the sharp tip of a steak knife.

Why had Lynn moved knives into this easy-access drawer, facing the blades the wrong direction, where Mattie or Lynn might hurt themselves?

I spun the phone around the room again, hoping my eyes had adjusted better to the faint illumination. Shadows swayed on the counters, a dance of unfamiliar shapes. The kitchen chairs appeared to have taller backs than usual, and one of the chairs seemed to have a person sitting in it. In a flicker of movement, the person began to rise.

I shifted my light source again and the person sat back down.

Apparently my mind was doing its best to make sense of limited and conflicting input, matching dark shapes with what I expected to be there. In that moment, I latched onto the only possible explanation: Somehow I'd stumbled into the wrong apartment. The similar floor plan tricked me into recognizing my own home, even when the furniture and appliances didn't match. No wonder I knocked over a vase. No wonder Lynn and the kids weren't here.

Although there wasn't anybody sitting in the dark kitchen, I spoke to the chair anyway—excused myself, apologized for the intrusion.

I moved back toward the entryway, my hand against the wall to guide me. The apartment didn't smell like home. I noticed baby powder and the fake fruity odor of those lip balms popular with teenage girls. Nearing the front door, I stepped carefully to avoid the shards of broken vase.

Then I heard a loud thumping on the ceiling. An unmistakable, heavy tread across the floor upstairs.

Mr. Stompy.

I guess that inconsiderate jerk finally did me a favor, helping me realize I was in the right apartment after all. It all came back to me. Lynn had ordered an imitation jade vase to place on an accent table next to the entryway closet. She'd mentioned last week how she planned to reorganize the kitchen drawers. And the latest kitchen contraption—a yogurt maker or egg boiler, wasn't it?

No doubt about it now, I was home. But still, where had my family gone? I tried to think where they might wander in a crisis. What neighbors did Lynn mention as friends? Would she have headed to the leasing office? Or to our car, to drive somewhere nearby?

I needed to figure out the quickest way to find them. I needed—

Thump, thump, thump.

I don't quite know how to explain, but I had this overwhelming need to find my family. It's not like I feared they were in danger—at least not yet. It was more like the sensation that *I* might be in danger if I didn't find them soon. But it was so dark, and I didn't know which way to—

Thump, thump, thump.

And goddamn, it was like a switch flipped in my brain. I was trying to think, but I couldn't concentrate with all that angry stomping overhead. So intrusive, disturbing my peace at any hour of the day, and this was the last time, the *last* time I was going to put up with it. Sure, I know what I just said, how my concern for my wife and kids was *everything*, so logically I shouldn't have let him distract me. Priorities, right? But maybe that's why I got so mad—crisis time, you know, and there he was being his usual inconsiderate self. A nuclear bomb could go off in the next town, shock waves of radiation headed our way, and he'd keep stomping from one room to the next.

So yeah, I decided to go upstairs and give him a piece of my mind. I'd bang on his door louder than his stupid elephant tread, scream at him when he answered, maybe even punch him—if he wasn't too old and feeble, like Lynn said. But he couldn't be that frail and have such malicious strength in his legs.

Thump, thump, thump.

Right. I'll give him something to stomp about.

I stepped outside our apartment, went to the dark stairs, grabbed the rail for guidance, and headed to the floor above.

THE STAIRS crunched beneath my feet. I knelt down in the dark to figure out what I was stepping on and found a layer of dried leaves. Someone must have opened the window on the landing and the leaves had blown through.

I crunched up the rest of the steps and felt my way to Stompy's door. Before I could bang on it, I noticed an odd ripple in the wood. I held the phone steady and brought its light close to the door, but nothing reflected back. When I reached out to knock, my hand went right through. The door was open and a thin, dark curtain enclosed the entrance.

Black crepe streamers, taped to the top of the doorframe.

When I walked through, the streamers parted and brushed against me. It felt like the air itself reached for me with gentle black tentacles.

A flickering light greeted me from the main room. Candles placed on tables and windowsills cast an unsteady glow.

The first thing I noticed was the carpet underfoot. Brown thin carpet like the kind you find in a library or a school. No padding underneath, so nothing to muffle footsteps.

A dark pattern stained a large portion of the carpet.

Thump, thump, thump.

At the center of the stain, a man sat in a chair. He seemed like the same man I'd imagined in the kitchen chair in our own apartment—a kind of rounded body, poised to stand but frozen in position.

"I need you to give me some peace." I walked toward him, my feet landing gently on his carpet as if to prove a reasonable step was possible. "We can hear you downstairs, always stomping around. It's like having a marching band living above us."

The candles flickered. The man's head turned toward me.

Thump, thump.

A balding head, but he didn't seem as old as the man Lynn described to me earlier. His jaw jutted out in a strange shape, and a metal-gray fabric glimmered in the candlelight.

Duct tape. A rag stuffed in his mouth, then covered and the tape wrapped around his head several times. Whoever taped his mouth must have also tied him to the chair.

Thump, thump.

Then the shape of his huddled body resolved itself. He wasn't sitting in a chair. He was a short, stocky man, stooped over in agony.

His bare feet were nailed to the floor.

He lifted one of his arms slightly. The effort was an incredible strain to him and his hand looked swollen and heavy like a bowling ball.

It dropped to the carpet and I heard the familiar thump-stomp. The other arm lifted and fell. The pattern repeated.

His large, round hands were orange and they grinned at me with wide jagged teeth.

Plastic jack-o'-lanterns for collecting Halloween candy. His hands have been placed in them, the containers filled with plaster or cement to weigh them down.

When did the sounds change? How long ago did they shift from an inconsiderate bounding across the floor into an agonized drumbeat for help?

"I'll get you some help. Mister, uh…" I didn't slip and call him by the nickname. "I'll get help."

I moved closer and he thumped his pumpkin hands on the thin carpet, and his eyes pleaded with me. He looked like he wanted to back away. As if he thought I was going to hurt him.

"Hey, no, I'm not going to hit you or anything. You mind if I borrow this? I'm going to get help."

I'd lifted a white candle from the nearby end table. The same kind of generic emergency candle we used to keep in our kitchen drawer, set in a tea saucer to keep the wax from dripping everywhere.

"Be back soon. Promise."

I HELD my free hand to protect the candle flame as I stepped through the streamers hanging from his doorframe. I couldn't help but think of old black-and-white movies as I headed toward the stairs—you know, those ones where rain-soaked travelers explore an empty mansion at night and later discover it's not so empty? They head down a spiral staircase, candelabra in one hand, brushing away cobwebs with the other. A rat scurries across their path and an owl hoots through the window.

No rat or owl here, but a rubber bat hung suspended from the ceiling. It bounced on an elastic string as I ducked under it, then I stepped through the dead leaves and dry twigs that someone had scattered along the stairs.

On the next level, the door to our apartment was wide open. I'd probably left it that way when I ran out but couldn't quite remember. Maybe my wife and kids had returned? I called their names and my voice echoed, the way sounds always seem to do in the dark.

No response.

In my mind's eye, I pictured them with duct tape around their mouths. They were locked in closets, tied in chairs. Their feet were nailed to the floor, their hands nailed to the wall or bound by chains or heavy plaster. They were crying and I knew I was close. If only I could hear them.

"Tap the wall," I said. "Kick something. Help me find you."

Nothing.

Then, to my relief, a muffled laugh. The sound carried from the ground-floor entrance, somewhere from the other side of the front door. Hard to pinpoint, but I knew it was my kid. Funny that I can't say if it was Mattie or Amber, but a parent knows the sounds his own kid makes. And I say laugh, because it had that kind of sputtering sound, like a hand over the mouth at church, maybe even during a funeral, where you're supposed to stay serious and can't help yourself. That kind of laugh.

In a rush of adrenaline, keeping the candle steady, I hurried downstairs and outside.

YOU'RE SAYING, "Why didn't you *this*, why didn't you *that*?"

Right?

You're thinking I should have searched my own apartment more thoroughly, now that I had the candle. Or I should have banged on neighbors' doors asking for their phone, at the top of my voice shouting, "Nine-one-one, somebody call nine-one-one!" Or even earlier, I should have taken the gag off the old guy's mouth to let him explain what happened.

These are easy questions to ask now. I wonder the same things myself sometimes.

Here's what I can tell you: In the moment, I was deep in the logic of dreams. Whatever happens, wherever it leads, you just have to go with it. It's like you're on rails.

I was on a child's funhouse rail car. The car was shaped like a coffin.

Which is not to say I was actually dreaming, although that's how it still feels to me now. This is simply how I remember what happened to me that Halloween night. You guys are supposed to understand things about dreams, so I'll let you be the judge.

All I can do is describe the rest of the ride.

LYNN

THIS IS goodbye for now, Mr. Therapist.

Things are much worse than I could ever have expected.

I'm beginning to think that Matt's been playing me the whole time.

Him and Amber, too.

Everything he's tried to hide from me and from Harris?

Well, let's just say I don't think he's tried to hide them from his sister.

And the fact that Amber never thought to break his confidence?

That she never got frightened enough to tell her mother or father?

And that she still loves her brother, despite what she must know?

That makes her just as bad.

I fear I've done exactly what they wanted all along. It's like they knew I was watching them, and they tricked me.

They wanted to stay home on Halloween day.

They wanted me to chase them outside.

So they'd have more time to prepare.

Now I have to go searching for them and try to stop them, and I'm not sure what to do with this file.

It was supposed to help me work through problems in my marriage.

Turns out I had bigger problems, right under my nose the whole time.

Maybe things will work out.

Therapy. It's helped me, so maybe it can help my kids.

I'm not going to say that they're too far gone.

A mother can't ever admit that, can she? She definitely can't type it in a document for all the world to see.

I won't delete this file just yet, since I may need to come back and tell you more, but I'll password-encrypt it.

I always knew I couldn't trust Harris.

Maybe I haven't been the best parent in the world, either.

I should never have let those kids out of my sight.

I'm going to find them now.

HARRIS   X

OUTSIDE, COOL air rippled through my hair and shook the candle flame into violent contortions. The late evening seemed, for lack of a better description, more *Halloween* than before. The moon emerged from the cover of clouds to cast a blue-gray glow on the surroundings. No other light, either from streetlamps or from apartment windows. No signs of life. A quiet, expectant calm—as if, any moment, a sinister evensong would rise and hooded monks would emerge between buildings, the leader cradling a small wrapped bundle in one arm, while his assistant prepared the ritualistic dagger.

Across the street, strips of orange crepe paper hung from an oak tree—tossed through the dry limbs the way tricksters might toss rolls of toilet paper to decorate a treatless home. The streamers rustled in the wind like flames.

The building I just left seemed older in this light, its bricks more like the illusion of stonework, crumbling toward ruin. The building next door, slightly larger, loomed over with the impression I'd always had: a big brother, one protective arm around his sibling. The buildings were stone golems, now. The bigger building looked ready to push the weaker one over, then trample it into the ground.

I ignored the sidewalk and crossed the grass to the concrete porch of the neighboring building. I pushed open the door and walked into the common lobby.

A grinning jack-o'-lantern sat atop each newel post at the bottom of the main stairway and a candle in each hollowed gourd supplemented my own light source. The notice board next to the mailboxes had been vandalized. Someone had broken off the Plexiglas front and placed rubber spiders and a giant rubber rat inside. Shawna's latest flyer hung where I'd pinned it—but someone had crossed out most of the rules. In heavy black marker, a ^NOT was added to THIS YEAR'S HALLOWEEN PARTY IS ^ CANCELED.

As with my building, leaves littered the lobby tile and the stairway. Some broken branches here, as well, and a few stones. A rubber snake lay half buried among the leaves, and the movement of my candlelight made its body slither as I passed.

The door to the Durkinses' ground-floor apartment was open, so I knocked on the doorframe as I crossed the threshold and called out for Marie or Todd.

"Sorry the power's gone out," I said. "Are you here?"

And damned if that freaking bird didn't squawk in answer. Louder than ever but the same distinctive and annoying cry.

Harris, it seemed to say. *Harris, I know you're there.*

In their living room, the Durkinses kept a gold-plated stand the height of a hat-rack, curved at the top and holding a suspended birdcage. A black cloth lay over the cage.

I crossed the living room, my way illuminated by various scented candles on the coffee table and on the mantel. The cloth hung loose on the dome-shaped cage, and I reached for a low flap to pull it away.

Fix this, Harris. Fix this!

The voice startled me, and I drew back my hand.

Stupid ugly fucker. Smelly bastard.

Those last phrases were some of the gems I'd whispered to the door when the Durkinses weren't home. The prank didn't seem so funny now, my crude phrases echoed back in a loud, robotic squawk. Whenever I'd attempted this trick, I'd been laughing outside their door. Any semblance of laughter was lost in the malicious threat of this new voice.

Go to hell, prick!

And then the bird *did* laugh, or at least mimic the sound as best it could. A poor simulation, empty of soul or feeling. The most sinister sound I'd ever heard.

I wasn't sure what animal had actually cooked in our family's stove, but I wanted this creature to share its fate. I tugged at the cloth and it fell away.

An enormous raw turkey filled the cage. It had been pressed in so tightly that the pink-and-white plucked skin bulged between the metal bars. The bone of a drumstick pressed against the small wire door, as if attempting to open it.

The cage rattled and I nearly convinced myself the thing inside was alive, trying to escape. It was awful and pink like a belly shaking with laughter. That sinister robotic laugh sounded again, so loud it filled the entire room. I held my candle still, suspecting the shake of my hand had caused an illusion of movement, but the cage continued to sway and rattle.

Then a section of pink, raw breast began to swell outward. A chittering and gnawing accompanied the motion, and then something wet and brown broke through from beneath the skin. Small yellow teeth appeared, and a stray wire or whisker or antenna waved through the opening.

In revulsion, I kicked the base of the cage stand, knocking the whole thing to the floor. I heard the squeak of tiny hinges and more of the chittering and gnawing before I raced out the door.

Or, in my metaphor from earlier, before the railcar of my carnival ride started up again, to deliver me to the next attraction.

I RAN up the stairs, my feet crunching over dead leaves, until I reached apartment 6C, where the college girl lived. Her name was Jessica something or other and I didn't really know her, although I had worked on her apartment a few times. She was another new resident, having just moved in before the current semester started.

The door to her apartment was open a crack and I pushed it the rest of the way. I had a vague memory of what she looked like, but I wouldn't have recognized her the way I found her.

The smell hit me first, even before my eyes focused on the horror before me. The stomach-turning stench reminded me of the time as a kid when my father forgot about a chicken breast he was grilling and we came back to find it burning to a crisp on the grate over the jumping flames. Only this wasn't a burned chicken.

Strung up from the ceiling fan was a body that I presumed had to be the college student. There were no real identifying features left. The corpse was charred black, almost as if this thing wasn't even human to begin with. Yet somehow the outfit that had been placed onto the burned body horrified me even more.

Her killer had dressed her in a sexy pirate costume, something she might have worn to a frat party for Halloween. There was an eyepatch over one of the charred eye sockets, a colorful striped dress, a headscarf, and a vest that resembled a corset. A bright plastic parrot perched on one shoulder.

As additional ornaments, dozens of blank CDs were pinned to the corpse and a typing keyboard was hanging from her neck.

There was also a handmade cardboard sign pinned to her body. Written on it in marker was:

Internet Piracy is NOT a Victimless Crime! Para-tweet!

I turned and ran before the vomit reached the top of my throat.

ANOTHER FRIGHT greeted me on the stairs. On the section between the second and third floors, a dead man lay along the slanted path. The body had been chopped to pieces, and all the pieces were connected with twine, allowing the man to stretch the full length of the staircase: his head lay sideways on the landing, the torso began a few steps down; the upper arms, then the forearms, then the hands below the middle step. The clothes had been cut, too, each portion of business suit matching the appropriate body part. Below the pelvis and leg segments, severed feet were laced into a pair of black Rockports.

The dead man's tongue bulged out of his mouth, and one of the eyes had been poked through. He had short, straight hair and a Vandyke beard peppered with gray. The private detective. This was the dead man I'd discovered previously in the empty apartment.

He looked twelve feet tall, simultaneously monstrous and ridiculous, like a marionette that had been drawn and quartered. Or like a child's disproportionate drawing during a game of hangman, the body parts overly distinguished to mark each incorrectly guessed letter.

To make my way up the stairs, I had to step around the body parts, careful not to catch my foot on the connecting twine.

I didn't bother going into the private detective's former surveillance office. Instead, I went to Joanne Huff's unit. Her door was closed and I waited for a moment outside, expecting her to sense my presence, as she often did.

Harris, I told you things would get worse. I insist you turn that power back on right away. I know you're there, now hurry up.

"Joanne? Mrs. Huff? I'm coming in." The knob turned easily and I opened the door and stepped inside.

Candles illuminated the living room, as had been the case with the other prepared apartment, the other decorated "stops" on this haunted attraction ride. Plain white candles lined the control panel for a bulky exercise treadmill. Two other candles sat like horns atop a football, a jack-o'-lantern face drawn onto the pigskin. Similarly decorated sports equipment littered the floor: volleyballs and basketballs and shuttlecocks, tennis racquets and balls, a jump rope, a pogo stick, and a pair of stilts. An exercise bike was positioned near the window, with a Ping-Pong table where Joanne's television used to sit. Completing the tableau: a full set of free weights, lined up according to size.

All of these items, no doubt retrieved from our activity closet in building two, seemed to crowd in an expectant circle around Joanne's mustard-colored lounge chair. They tempted her, called to her to rise and push her body to its limits, to play, to set goals, to enjoy the pleasures of an active life.

Her chair was turned away toward the window now instead of the false window of the television. On her end table, a manila envelope lay open, and several upturned pill bottles. The pills themselves were no-where in sight.

I had a sudden urge to kick the basketball at my feet. Its upturned pumpkin face seemed especially crude and smug, and I imagined the ball sailing through the air, the candle flames spinning.

Instead, I stepped over the ball, set my own candle on the Ping-Pong table as I reached for the back of Joanne's chair.

She had to be in that chair. She couldn't possibly be anywhere else.

"You called me about a smell." My hand touched the puffed top of the chair back and I could almost feel taut muscle beneath the vinyl skin. "The smell of death. It's getting worse, you said."

I couldn't stop myself, despite how much I dreaded what I might find. I pulled and the chair began to swivel to face me. From behind, I saw the terrycloth cap she wore to cover unwashed hair. The chair turned, I saw stray tufts of hair, but the wing of the chair covered her face. *Stop turning,* I thought, *Please,* but the motion was under way, too late to stop, and an odor wafted up.

It smelled like illness. Like *her.*

The chair turned, but Joanne's legs didn't dangle from the seat. Instead, two molasses smears trailed over the cushions and to the floor. The sludge poured out the bottom cuffs of her flower-print pajamas.

A television remote sat on one arm of the chair. Atop the remote lay five slug shapes—a gelatinous hand, too weary to adjust the controls. Attached to the hand, more thick sludge led to a sleeve of her cardigan.

Pressed into the syrup, I noticed small flecks of hair similar to those I'd previously seen on Joanne's arm.

Her face. God, how I dreaded looking where her face should be.

It was stuck to the chair, a congealed bas-relief above the open neck of her sweater, with bristle-wisps of hair and her terry-cloth cap on top. A hint of facial features remained in the sludge: eyebrows like caterpillars; the bulge of her nose and a button of mole on her cheek; two plump lines suggesting the fullness of her lips.

Her eyes were closed, as if asleep. In the flicker of candlelight, her features appeared to move—a slight raise of her brow, a sudden pucker of the mouth.

As I backed away in revulsion, my heel crushed something rubbery. A tennis ball, I think, but it felt like I'd stepped on an ingredient fallen from the soup in the chair: a piece of lung or stomach or kidney. I swung my arms for balance, but instead of falling backward I overcorrected and fell forward.

Toward the chair.

As my feet slipped from under me, I made the mistake of opening my mouth to cry out.

I turned my head but not soon enough. I landed against the sludge face. Gelatin lips smeared across my mouth and onto my cheek, and a thick sickly odor forced its way up my nostrils. As I pulled away, part of her face clung to my own. I tasted her illness, and it was cancer and scurvy and rot; it was spite and selfishness and cruelty, seasoned into the sludge of inactivity. Most vile of all, a hint of sweetness flavored the syrup, like the insult of peppermint deodorizer in the ward of the dying.

Wiping my lips with the back of my hand, spitting the diseased taste from my mouth, I raced out of the room.

I'd forgotten my candle, but enough others had been placed in the hallway to light my way. On the stairway, I slowed through the obstacle course of the detective's stretched body. One misstep and I'd have pulled the tangle of twine and limbs along with me.

All I wanted to do now was wash my face and hands. I'd almost forgotten about my missing wife and children. I felt unworthy of them, my face coated with a layer of someone else's hatred and illness.

The rooms I'd already entered were off-limits. I'd already experienced those horrors, and the carnival ride would not let me retrace my path. On the second floor, I went into the unit across the hall from the college girl's apartment.

A sink with running water. That's all I wanted. Plus some gristled soap and a scouring pad to scratch at my face and hands. Bleach, if necessary.

I decided to head straight to the kitchen, avoiding any spook-house scares in the living room. Whatever was positioned there, however the body was propped up or mutilated or transformed, I wouldn't look.

I wouldn't...

But curiosity got the best of me.

And maybe in the back of my mind, I'd convinced myself things couldn't get any worse.

This one. This one was so bad, I can't bring myself to describe all of it. I've described some pretty bizarre stuff already—so if I stop short here, that tells you something, doesn't it?

The apartment belonged to the Tammisimo family. Their kid, Andrew, was kind of the ringleader of a group of teenagers in our community. "Gang" might be the better word, if they had any sense of organization or purpose. But really, all they did was hang out, maybe make snide comments as you passed but quick to back down if you challenged them. *Oh, we didn't say nothing, Naylor. Just chillin'.* All talk, with no muscle to back it up: of the four of them, two were spindly thin, one was stocky and short, and the other was a slightly plump girl who followed them more out of inertia than interest. Tyler was the short one, and he'd basically latched on to the three rare people he thought he could boss around.

I always suspected they were the ones who bent back the fence to make a shortcut off our property. If supplies went missing, if a window got broken or if spray paint appeared on a brick wall, any one of them might be the culprit.

But I'd never once thought to blame them for what was happening now. Not enough imagination among the four of them combined. No sense of purpose, like I said. Even if one of them came up with an idea, they'd be collectively too lazy to follow through.

The Tammisimo apartment proved my instincts correct. The main room was heavily vandalized—smashed furniture, broken glass. Torn wallpaper and harsh black letters written on the walls.

The four teenagers were piled in the middle of the floor, and their bodies had been vandalized, too. That's the part I can't bring myself to describe. Even in the dim candlelight, I saw too much. Not just how their bodies had been broken, but how they'd been reassembled. How they'd been cut open, and what was put inside them.

And those words on the wall. Not words, exactly, but the shape of words and sentences, in some alphabet I couldn't recognize.

Commands.

A demon alphabet of spirals and hideous angles, lines crossing torn wallpaper and battered drywall, a breeze contorting the letters, candle flames making them dance. If I stared long enough, they'd twist into familiar shapes. I'd be able to translate the phrases, understand what they asked me to do.

MY HYPOTHETICAL coffin-shaped rail car continued to guide me, and I prayed I was nearing the end of the ride. I longed for the moment when my car would burst through a swinging set of wooden doors into the bright outdoors. I would laugh, the way people always laughed after a funhouse ride, and that would prove I'd never really been scared, that every room was filled with mannequins and mechanical effects, the atmosphere supplied by painted backdrops and strobe lights and tape-recorded screams.

Downstairs seemed the logical ending to the ride. I followed the leaf-strewn steps to the basement floor, with the supply room and laundry facility, and with the community meeting space that hosted all our major events, including the previous years' Halloween parties.

And this year's party, too—back on the schedule, if the hand-altered flyer could be believed.

Outside the locked storage room, strategically placed candles revealed my toolkit on the floor where I'd left it. Someone had replaced the tools with Halloween treats—Red Hots, chocolate kisses, candy corn, and colorful gumballs—all loose from their wrappers, as if to assist the poisoner's efforts. Plastic goblin fingers reached from beneath the pile, poised to close around the wrists of greedy children. A glint of metal flashed here and there: razor blades or straight pins.

No sign of my heavy-duty Maglite, but a dollar-store replacement lay beside the toolkit. This plastic flashlight was orange with a pumpkin-shaped dome on the end. When I picked it up and pushed the switch, the jack-o'-lantern face lit up and a focused beam shone out the hollow top of the pumpkin's head.

Better than nothing. At the time, I was grateful for the improved visibility.

With what came next, I'd rather have been blind.

THE DOORS to the activity room were both shut. A full-sized effigy of a hanged witch dangled in front of the entrance. The rope was tied to the door handle, threaded up to a pulley in the ceiling, and the noose was looped over the dummy's neck.

An interesting historical fact, Mattie. They didn't actually burn witches at the stake in Salem. They hanged them. And then I'd added as a joke: *Though a fire is nice sometimes, right?*

Black frizzy hair fell wild beneath the pointed witch's cap. Her rubber skin was green and wide eyes were painted on her face. A large wart balanced at the end of her crooked nose.

The body was draped by a full black robe with wadded newspapers or straw holding the shape beneath. A piece of paper was fastened to the front of the robe, but I couldn't quite distinguish the writing on it. I aimed the flashlight at the note and walked closer.

My face and hands were still sticky, and a rotten taste had settled in the back of my throat. I felt a gust of damp basement air and watched how the body swung in the breeze.

It didn't sway like a robe stuffed with paper or straw. There was more heft to the body, maybe like a plaster store mannequin beneath the clothing. Not a real body. Surely not a real body.

Because the shape in the robe seemed suddenly familiar.

It bore an unsettling resemblance to how my wife might look if she floated above the floor, a rubber mask over her head and the life strangled out of her.

As I reached forward, I hoped for a crinkle of newspaper or straw when I touched the robe, rather than the soft give of a woman's torso. My hand hovered over the attached note, which I was now close enough to read.

Large bold letters, like the message a killer tapes to a body for the police to find: SHE CANCELED HALLOWEEN.

I lay my palm against the front of the black, flowing costume, then pushed.

And God help me, the body felt heavy. And the way it moved…

I knew it had to be Lynn. Hadn't my wife said those same words, about canceling Halloween? I wanted to hug her, untie the rope, then get her down, lift the mask and breathe life back into her. My wife and I had some problems lately, but nothing that couldn't be fixed. I loved her. Our children needed her.

Standing on tiptoes, I reached up for the mask. My fingers brushed against the coil of noose. I slipped them under the warm flap of latex and felt human skin beneath. Was this the neck I used to caress? The neck I'd lay gentle fingertips upon in the middle of the night, when Lynn slept so soundly I feared her heart had stopped beating, and I'd wait, wait for the reassuring pulse that always came?

No pulse.

The hat fell over and toppled to the floor. I grabbed the mask and began to pull at it like peeling the skin off someone's face.

Not Lynn's face. It can't be my wife.

And I made a deal then, with God or whatever devil ruled that Halloween night.

If Lynn has died, change what happened. Take it all back.

I'll give you someone else.

Because didn't she and my wife have similar figures, indistinguishable beneath a robe and mask? Even a husband can be fooled.

The pieces clicked in my mind. *It's perfect! She canceled Halloween, too!*

The idea made sense. It could have been Shawna's corpse all along. Didn't matter that I never much liked my boss. She still made a worthy sacrifice.

I convinced myself these vile thoughts were noble rather than selfish. A wish born out of love, a heroic attempt at keeping my family together.

Take Shawna.

Hang her instead.

The mask fell off easily, and I crumpled it in my hand.

I GRABBED the door handle. A knotted rope was still attached, though the noose now dangled empty from the ceiling. I pulled open the door, then entered the assembly room.

It was like walking into a cave. This windowless half of the large room, the section directly beneath the apartment building, had typical basement features: wood-paneled walls, industrial carpet, and thick concrete support pillars at regular intervals. The far half of the room, which extended beyond the building at the back, opened into a higher ceiling and featured aboveground windows along the perimeter. The shutters remained closed, the windows covered with black and orange cloth. Black streamers of varying length draped from the ceiling, and they rolled like waves among other scattered decorations. Paper cutouts of ghosts, skeletons, vampires.

Frankenstein's monster, a werewolf, witches on brooms. More pumpkins and bats and owls. Several ropes dangled down, each empty noose inviting a fresh guest. A few of them were already occupied, ropes pulled tight over the plastic necks of baby dolls.

Despite the many lit candles—along the floor, on scattered chairs, on every tabletop—the room remained dark. The ends of a few streamers dangled near a flame, as if straining toward oblivion. I remember having a morbid thought that Shawna was lucky not to be here. She would never have allowed the potential fire hazard.

She wouldn't have allowed this party, either.

The food setup matched that of previous years, with two long tables on each side for cake and candy, and a punch bowl at the far end. But the middle seating area had changed. Instead of chairs arranged around banquet tables, with a space up front cleared for dancing and games and the costume contest, the chairs had been placed in rows with an aisle down the middle. Kind of like a church.

People sat in every chair. Almost a hundred, by my quick estimate, which was a good percentage of the community residents—possibly with some of their guests in tow. How had news of the event spread so quickly?

I moved closer, trying to locate my kids. I aimed the flashlight to supplement the weak glow from the candles. Hands went up to cover faces as my beam passed over.

The people all wore masks, as was proper for Halloween. But the partygoers also wore black hoods over their heads, with long robes covering the rest of their costumes. I could barely distinguish the adults from the children.

One shape on the right edge seemed the approximate size of Mattie or Amber. I moved closer and waved my beam beneath the hood, and protesting hands covered the eye holes of a goblin mask. The rubber hands sported thick black hair and yellow talons.

"Mattie?"

The hooded head shook back and forth. "Go away."

"It's your father," I said.

A rubber hand reached into the hood, lifted the bottom of the mask to reveal the person's mouth. "You're nobody's father." The figure spoke in a deep voice that didn't match the child's frame. A full red beard surrounded his mouth.

I heard a stifled snort a few seats over. "Where's your costume, Naylor?" A robed figure elbowed a person on his left who was doubled over as if laughing. The mocking questioner reminded me of Andrew Tammisimo, emboldened by the presence of his pathetic friends.

But I'd seen what happened to all four of them, how their bones had been snapped, how their skin was cut and stretched and rearranged, and how those writhing *things* had been pressed inside their opened bodies...

As I stepped back from the goblin dwarf, I bumped against one of the long food tables. My hand pressed down into a piece of cake or pie, and an awful custard oozed between my fingers.

What kind of food might be served at such a gathering? I imagined gelatin molded in the shape of a brain and hard-boiled eggs with eyes painted on them. Cupcakes with black icing and cookies shaped like pumpkins and ghosts. The punch, of course, would be red; something small and hairy would swim through it.

A large shape rose above the nearest section of the table. Though it had been transformed, I recognized the structure instantly: Amber's dollhouse, turned into a haunted centerpiece. The white siding with pink shutters had been painted over with black and gray, simulating a dilapidated mansion. In the cutaway rooms, most of the tiny furniture was broken, and the little walls were covered in grime. Instead of doll men and women, several large cockroaches scurried across the miniature floors, tiny action-figure heads glued to their backs. A legless mouse, with a makeshift leash tied tight around its torso, writhed on an upstairs bed. A salted slug trailed over the kitchen stove and over tiny plastic plates and pans.

Instead of curtains, cut sections of flypaper adorned the windows. Insects coated the sweet glue, and the paper rustled from the buzz and wing flaps of those alive enough to struggle.

The whole thing was like a grade-school diorama project gone horribly wrong. But Amber loved her dollhouse—the prettiness of it, the delicate small things. She never would have altered it like this.

I thought again of the nearby food and of the insects on the flypaper. The residue of custard on my fingers now seemed to crawl with life.

A new sound chittered from a row near the front: the clack of fingers on a computer keypad. It reminded me of the college girl in 6C, how I never heard her voice if I listened outside her door but always heard that frantic tap and click, a sad attempt to connect with the world. If I'd visited her in the middle of the night, I probably would have heard the same thing.

My broken cellphone began to ring and vibrate in my pocket. More heads turned, as if I'd violated etiquette at a movie or a funeral. I pressed down, feeling glass break against the fabric of my pocket.

Joanne Huff's voice emerged from the phone: *It's getting worse, Harris. It's everywhere.* Her voice was loud but muffled, like someone speaking from behind a mask.

Perhaps she didn't speak from my phone at all. She could have been any one of these masked attendees.

It occurred to me that they might all be here. All the people who died in their apartments.

Their violent deaths gave their spirits extra power. They possessed the living and spoke through them. On this special night of the year, their ghosts assumed earthly form.

Some of these people were my neighbors. Some of them were unholy monsters.

There was no way to tell them apart.

All the seated figures faced the front now, ignoring me, but I still couldn't shake the feeling of being watched. In the gloom amid the streamers and decorations and candles, I searched for the red glowing eyes of surveillance cameras. The cameras all pointed at me, waiting to see what I would do.

Then a figure stood from the front row and stepped forward. The figure turned to face the audience, and an expectant murmur rose from the crowd.

This person wore the same hooded robe as the others but stood with a commanding posture that suggested leadership. Something about the shape suggested a woman's form to me—similar to the witch I'd seen in the noose outside the room.

Two smaller figures stood from the front row and stepped to either side of her. They didn't turn around.

The woman raised her hands to her hood and began to pull it back.

I thought it might be Lynn, it might be Shawna, but I couldn't distinguish any features. She wasn't wearing a mask, but her face wouldn't settle into focus.

She made a gesture with her finger, pointing to herself, then to the crowd, and it was similar to the "You and me" motion I used to make with my wife. But it had a horrible beckoning quality, too—as if it was an invitation to participate in something awful.

The smaller figures on either side of her kept their backs to me. I was pretty sure I knew who they were.

A chant now filled the hushed room. The song was low and somber, and the words didn't make any sense. It was like a hymn in a foreign language. A dead language.

I blinked and glowing letters seemed to dance in front of my eyes. The twisted letters took obscene shape like the demonic phrases scrawled on the wall of the upstairs room.

The letters flickered red and hot.

They spelled my name. And they spelled "fire." And they spelled "now."

Several black streamers hung low near my face. I pulled one of them and the pleated paper stretched slightly. I brought it toward a tall orange candle on the nearby table.

Flame caught the end of the streamer, and I let the paper go. It bounced back in place, swinging a small arc over the crowd and toward other hanging papers.

The fire spread to the tall ceiling. As the streamers burned, sections broke off and rained fire and ash over the people seated below.

The crowd continued to chant their tragic hymn.

☠

YOU KNOW the rest, probably better than me, especially since I can't remember where the real events end and where the fictional mixed-up world of my reoccurring nightmares begin.

Even if you won't give me all of the facts, everyone knows it couldn't have happened the way it does in the nightmares.

But everyone did burn, right?

That part was real, wasn't it? It had to be. Just look at my hands.

They all burned, right?

All the residents of Stillbrook Apartments, including my wife and children.

They all burned.

Didn't they?

THE FINAL INTERVIEW

HE'S DIFFERENT than I expect. Older and worn down, the way time in such a place can alter a man's grooming habits and posture. A person's pride slips away, along with his inner spirit.

The medications typically don't help. Per my request, they've limited Naylor's dosage today to keep him alert.

The previous director at the Klinenberg facility, Sylvia Jeffers, had severely restricted Naylor's access to facts uncovered in subsequent investigations for fear such details might confirm the patient's delusions. She and her team essentially kept Naylor in a bubble with no access to media reports and strict instructions on what visitors could and could not say. Thomas Edgeworth, newly appointed, has granted me far more leeway than his predecessor. He's allowed the investigation to take precedence. To his way of thinking, uncovering the truth, facing it directly, should benefit all parties.

On the various recordings he's made, Naylor doesn't provide a full explanation. However, in most occurrences that seem to incriminate the children, he offers an excuse or diversion—sometimes casting suspicion on himself, more frequently on his deceased wife. A few sections seem to incriminate the community manager, Shawna Diedrichs, but that seems a red herring.

His voice is instantly familiar, the way a celebrity's might be. I've listened to his recordings over and over: I know his cadences, the way he speeds up when he's ready to make a wry comment, how he'll drop to a slow whisper when he describes something ominous or terrifying.

His voice is also familiar like an old friend's. Though he addresses the therapist du jour on each segment, he achieves an easy rapport throughout most of the narrative and even a disinterested listener could get drawn into his story.

In all fairness, I could hardly call myself disinterested.

The most startling aspect of his appearance, to me, is his hands. Whatever surgery they were able to perform hasn't corrected the problem. In fact, multiple skin grafts seem to have made those hands even more monstrous—and doubtless left wide scars on hidden parts of his body where the transplant skin had been borrowed. He wears no bandages to hide the damage received in the fire. Scars and red bumps cover his hands and his fingers are fused together.

But he still waves those hands in the air as he talks, as if they aid his expressiveness. He'd offered his right hand when I first stepped into the room, and it would have been impolite for me to refuse.

As we shook, it felt like I gripped a charred steak, crusted over and giving off excessive heat. In the medical portion of his file, a doctor notes Naylor's complaint that the nerve endings remain raw, and he suffers pain as if his hands are still on fire.

Several psychiatric evaluations interpret these complaints as psychosomatic.

Detective Stephens: Thanks for agreeing to meet with me.

Harrison Naylor: Didn't realize I had a choice. [Laughs.] Kidding. I wouldn't turn down any visitor. Every day here's pretty much the same, so it's nice to have company.

Stephens: I assume you don't object that I'm recording this?

Naylor: Fine, yeah. Oh, I catch your inference. I must be comfortable with voice recordings, since I made so many of them myself. Well, I couldn't very well write or type with [indicates his hands]…with these.

Stephens: You probably expect you'll get something out of this meeting as well. Answers.

Naylor: I was hoping you might fill in some gaps. That's what the new guy said, at least.

Stephens: I'll reveal what I can. But there's a process we'll need to fol—

Naylor: Oh, here we go.

Stephens: —need to follow. I *will* tell you things. I promise. But we have to talk first. I don't want the details in these folders to influence your initial comments.

Naylor: You've *got* my initial comments. Hours' and hours' worth. I've waited so long, and they tell me nothing here. Nothing. It's all word games and activity time, meals and pills and lights-out on schedule.

Stephens: I understand this has been frustrating for you. For me as well.

Naylor: For you. [Takes a long breath, is visibly calmer.] They taught me that here. Counting to ten.

Stephens: Good. I wanted to go through the different theories, if that's all right.

Naylor: Sure.

Stephens: Okay. Um. First, I guess, the theory that you did it yourself.

Naylor: Did *what*? I'm not trying to be cute here. I've had no confirmation of the events I described on those recordings. As if they never really happened, and hell, I'd probably like to believe that. Find a way to convince me. I won't resist.

Stephens: The fire, of course. You've already admitted some role in that. But also the alterations to apartments in buildings five and six, including the basement lounge. The decorations. The elaborate stagings. The bodies.

Naylor [an inappropriate relief, as if a weight has been lifted off his shoulders]: They never said. A fire, yeah, they couldn't hide that the fire happened. That my wife and kids are gone. But they never confirmed the other stuff.

Stephens [relenting]: I can confirm that now.

Naylor: The man on the stairs? The pirate girl?

Stephens [opening a folder, sliding photographs across the table]: The concrete construction of the basement helped shield the rest of the building from fire. Smoke damage, mostly.

Naylor [searches through the photos like viewing vacation shots; a kind of distracted excitement]: Here, just like I said. The thing in the birdcage. The sludge in Mrs. Huff's chair. My upstairs neighbor guy, feet nailed to the floor and pumpkins on his hands.

Stephens: There's one I haven't shown you.

Naylor: [pause] The Tammisimo apartment. Those four teenagers. I don't want to see that one.

Stephens: Stay with me, Naylor. You asked for proof…

Naylor: Careful what you ask for. Right?

Stephens: We were discussing any role you played in these deaths. The fire at the end. You made that happen.

Naylor: I think so. Of everything, that seemed most like a dream. I remember the motion of my hand, grabbing the streamer and guiding it toward a candle. But maybe something coerced me. A voice in my head. They were all there? They all died?

Stephens: The whole community attended the Halloween party. You were the only survivor.

Naylor: And that automatically makes me guilty, I guess.

Stephens: How did you get out?

Naylor: I really don't know. I woke lying on the ground outside the building. The basement was in flames and the fire trucks began their work. Smoke everywhere, and I felt the heat on my face. On my hands.

Stephens: You mentioned being exhausted. Earlier that day, I mean. Your shoulder muscles ached and your hands were sore like you'd spent the day building things.

Naylor: Shawna's list. I did some plumbing work. I made a lot of shelves.

Stephens: And possibly some work with saws and knives. Redecorating. Moving equipment around. Tying knots.

Naylor: If I'd killed those people, if I'd made all the changes to their apartments, set the bodies up in that way, then why was each room a surprise when I entered? They shocked me. Horrified me. I'd have to have a split personality for that theory to make sense, and nobody's ever mentioned that possibility. Nothing like that in my files, is there?

Stephens: No. But you mentioned coercion before. A voice in your head. Some form of possession, maybe?

Naylor: Out of the question. I'd have known.

Stephens: You had access to all the storage rooms. A master key that opened every apartment.

Naylor: Shawna had that, too. Keys can be borrowed. Copied.

Stephens: Okay, then. How do you explain this? So many of the rooms contained references to things only you would know about. In-jokes with your family, like Mr. Stompy or Para-tweet.

Naylor: I've wondered about that, too.

Stephens: The ideas and images all came from your mind, to some extent. If you weren't responsible for the murders, for the changes to each apartment, then it was someone else hoping to cast suspicion your way. Or trying to send you a message. Someone who knew you best. Someone in your family.

Stephens: Which brings us to the second theory: that your wife was responsible.

Naylor: As a parent? We *both* were.

Stephens: No, I meant that she committed the murders herself.

Naylor: In my darkest moments, I might have believed that. I don't anymore.

Stephens: And yet, you mentioned how much she changed in those days leading up to Halloween. Setting up surveillance cameras, spying on her own kids. Her attitude toward you was different as well.

Naylor: Any relationship goes through rough patches. She was a good wife, and an even better mother. Really conscientious. Hard worker, too. They loved her at ComQues.

Stephens: Actually, she was fired.

Naylor: That's not true.

Stephens: October twenty-seventh. Immediate termination, including cutoff of her account access.

Naylor: But I overheard her using the headset, interacting with customers. She'd tell me about some of the calls in the evening, how she solved their network or software problems.

Stephens: I'm afraid that was a show, put on for your benefit.

Naylor: I can't believe it. She took such pride in her work…

Stephens: Your wife kept a kind of diary on her computer. We've been able to recover parts of the encrypted file. Look, uh. Is there any reason she might have been seeing a marriage counselor?

Naylor: What? Of course not. I've said we had a rough patch or two, like any couple. We were fine. We were always fine.

Stephens: I'm not exactly sure if she really did see a counselor. It's just that…

Naylor: Those printouts. Can I read them?

Stephens: I'll show you excerpts. They're written to a marriage counselor, presumably at the counselor's request. We can't locate the actual therapist, however.

[Stephens passes some pages. Pause while Naylor looks them over.]

Naylor [finished reading]: Look, this doesn't seem like her at all. Calling those kids "assholes." Yeah, that's a word I'd use, but Lynn? Never. And the way she threatens them?

Stephens: It doesn't fit your image of her.

Naylor: Not her at all. It couldn't be.

Stephens: Let me tell you why your wife was fired from her job. She used inappropriate language with customers. ComQues records their customer service calls, and they provided some examples.

[Click:]

Lynn Naylor (recording): I'm not going to put up with your shit much longer, understand? I know where you live. I have all the information I need to ruin your life.

[Click:]

Lynn Naylor (recording): Oh, you're crying like a baby now? You're one of those assholes who dish it out but can't take it. Well, fuck you.

[Click:]

Lynn Naylor (recording): To fix this problem, I need your permission to access your computer remotely. Can you click on "Yes" when the dialog window pops up? Great. But, oh, maybe you shouldn't have done that. I'm opening your image viewer. Here's a picture of a woman's throat being slit. It could be your wife. Let me increase the resolution for you. That's what will happen if you ever talk to me again like you did a few minutes earlier. Don't dare complain to my supervisor. I'll know if you do.

Naylor [stunned]: That's her. That's really her. She sounds like she's out of her mind.

Stephens: Your wife had access to your keys. She knew about all the other tenants. From conversations with you, she knew the in-jokes about Mr. Stompy and Joanne Huff and even the Durkinses' pet bird, and she could have altered each apartment accordingly.

Naylor: So you're saying it was Lynn. My wife was responsible for all of it.

Stephens: That's not what I'm saying at all. Your own account provides enough information to make your wife a plausible suspect. In the final gathering, you imply your wife is the hooded figure at the front of the crowd, a leader of some ominous ceremony. The situation with her employer adds further suspicion. That Mrs. Naylor was seeing a marriage therapist, or pretending to—either way—points to some imbalance in the household. All combined to push her over the edge. You're in the institution, but she was the crazy one.

Naylor: That's...[pause] I think that's right.

Stephens: You needed your wife as a plausible suspect. It's better than believing the alternative.

Better than suspecting your own children.

Naylor: No. Listen, I've covered this ground. I'm not afraid to face the possibility. It just never made sense. They're little kids. Good kids.

Stephens: You taught Mattie about Halloween. About hanging witches, versus burning them. About making your own Halloween displays, like you and your friends did at boarding school, decorating the dormitory despite the headmaster's wishes. Mattie and Amber grew close. They shared things you'd told them, and they overheard a good bit more. They learned things from...other sources. Let's consider the hanging man you found in the empty apartment. The private detective. I think he represented a kind of test run. To adopt your metaphor, it was an early attempt at the "first stop" of a haunted-house ride. That's why it didn't make sense. The lemon.

Naylor: I know what you're going to say. Again, they were little kids.

Stephens: The tableau was set to mimic autoerotic asphyxiation. Strangulation during self-pleasure, to heighten sensation. Those who practice it might put a lemon or lime in their mouth, and if they start to pass out, the main danger during this solitary practice, they'll bite down on the fruit wedge and the bitter taste will jolt them awake. In the bathroom of that empty apartment: A strangled body. A lemon nearby, as if some textbook mentioned it was necessary. But the rest of the scene's botched, since the man's trousers are fastened. It's like whoever put it together knew some of the ingredients but missed the big picture. Too *young* to understand what the man would actually be doing...

Naylor: Absurd.

Stephens: You just don't want to believe it. Obviously they put the bird in your oven. Mattie and Amber together, I'm guessing. Your wife was right to punish them equally. But she had another reason. She kept the children home on Halloween day, not—

Naylor: I explained that.

Stephens: —not from her choice, but because the kids had been suspended. In our post-Columbine culture, schools can't be too careful, even with little kids. Nobody knows where they got it, but Mattie and Amber brought an antique book to school. It described lurid rituals, featured photographs and diagrams of people being tortured or sacrificed. The main argument of the book was that violent deaths brought power—the more imaginative the deaths, the better. And for these to happen on Halloween...

Naylor: Where is this book?

Stephens: I hope it's been destroyed.

Naylor: All inference. You've got no real proof.

Stephens: Mattie's drawer. The locked drawer you set up for him. In your wife's diary, she mentions opening it. Being horrified at what she discovered. [Rustling of papers.] We found these drawings.

Naylor [unbelieving]: These are...These are...

Stephens: Blueprints, essentially. The man on the stairs. A bare foot, with an X marked where the nail should go. A partial list of chemicals that may have contributed to the liquefaction of Joanne Huff's body.

Naylor: These are...in Mattie's handwriting. His drawings, too, with help from Amber.

And these letters here...

Stephens: Not letters. They match the symbols painted over the Tammisimo's wallpaper.

Naylor: I still can't…It's impossible.

Stephens: It makes sense now, doesn't it? Despite your protests and excuses?

Naylor: No.

Stephens: The different apartments, your kids' fingerprints were all over them. And the way the knots were tied, as if by smaller hands. The knife cuts slanted at an upward angle, indicating someone standing low to the ground.

Naylor: I refuse to—

Stephens: Before the basement fire, two small robed figures stood at the front of the room, on either side of your wife. When they turned around…I know what you saw.

Naylor: You couldn't.

Stephens: Yes, I can. I've seen them, too.

　　—end of recording—

☠

I TURN off the recorder myself. I see how agitated Naylor was getting and I'm afraid of what might happen next.

He surprises me.

This man I'd come to know so well through studying his case, listening to his voice over and over, his confidence and cleverness and self-deception. So much bluster and personality, striving for an ironic detachment even at the edge of the most horrific discoveries.

Now, his eyes well up with tears.

"Mattie? Amber? You *saw* them?"

I nod in the affirmative. "Last Halloween."

"Oh." The catch in Naylor's voice really gets to me. It reminds me how much I love my own children. "They're alive."

"I'm afraid not."

Then I explain what happened in my own gated community last year. Out of concern for our children's safety, we'd also decided to curtail holiday celebrations. No exchanges of candy, no door-to-door trick-or-treating. We all agreed.

After dark, our doorbell rang.

I answered it. Two children stood on our front porch. They wore black robes, hoods pulled over their heads.

I began to explain the rules to them, when my wife came up behind me. "Oh, what's the harm," she said. She'd bought several bags of "fun-size" candy before the community's collective decision to cancel Halloween. She pulled open a sealed bag, then dropped small boxes of Runts and Bottle Caps into each of their plastic pumpkins. "Let's see your masks," she said.

The children pulled back their hoods.

The Halloween Children.

That night, so many of my neighbors died in their houses in ways too elaborate and horrible to explain. Yet a few families, like my own, were spared. I assume because we'd been the only ones to give them candy.

"I know what you saw," I tell Naylor. "Their masks. So realistic, like children with adult faces. Your own faces. Harris and Lynn Naylor."

I will never forgot how sinister they looked on our porch, at the threshold of our home. Adult expressions staring up from smaller robed figures, the angle wrong as if they stood in a deep pit, as if part of their bodies fell through the earth into a darker realm.

If Naylor revealed this detail to his therapists, they might have told him it was a displacement, a projection. He saw his own face on Mattie, Lynn's face on Amber, and that "dream image" represented how parents often feel responsible for their children's actions. You shape your children's view of the world, and you see yourself in them. In what they do.

You're all guilty. You're all the Halloween Children.

What created them? The tension in the home, the corrupting ideas that swarmed thick in the air, horrors disguised as entertainment. Distrust, competition, favoritism. Surveillance that expects to uncover the most vile behavior. Combine that with an ancient holiday, a strange isolated community, whatever ghosts and demons—literal or otherwise—linger in various rooms.

I don't tell him all these theories. I have a more important question.

"Assuming it is your children," I say, "do you know how we might stop them from coming back again next Halloween?"

He considers my question, his mind seeming to drift back over everything he described in his narrative, revising each section in light of what I've explained. He's calm now. He has accepted the truth.

His voice drops into that whisper now, the one he'd use on the tapes when his hand reached into uneasy darkness.

"You know how I treated my family," he says. "The favoritism I had for Mattie, which I couldn't help...but maybe I could have hidden it better. You probably know about my past, too, what I did to my parents before I left home, and why I was sent away to a special school. I remember it as an accident, and the police records support my version." He's actively crying as he continues. "Maybe if the bad stuff can just stay buried. If we could manage not to bring it forward, not to pass it along to our kids like poison, and they pass it to their kids, and on and on."

I'm genuinely moved. My own eyes well with tears, and I cross to his side of the table. Strange as he is, crazy as he is, I like this man.

"Maybe if we could just love our children," he said. "Love them."

I'm crying now, too. He stands and I give him a reassuring hug.

I feel a strange rub along my neck, the drag of a warm wet rag over my throat and a scratch like dry husks.

His scabbed-over hands, attempting to strangle me.

They have no grip, but he pushes them against my windpipe. I can feel several scabs pop and a warm thick liquid runs over my neck and down my collar.

I shove him away, scramble backward, and push the red emergency button on the wall. Harris Naylor begins to laugh.

"The Halloween Children," he says, and there's fear in his voice, and a parent's admiration, too.

He continues to laugh as the attendants rush into the room to subdue him.

-- end of manuscript --

Made in the USA
Monee, IL
16 September 2020

42724143R00132